SUP

Lock Down Publications and Cash
Presents

SUPER GREMLIN 3

Kut-Throat Business

By **KING RIO**

First Edition 2023

Printed in the United States of America

Lock Down Publications
P.O. Box 944
Stockbridge, GA 30281
www.lockdownpublications.com

Like our page on Facebook: Lock Down Publications
www.facebook.com/lockdownpublications.ldp

Stay Connected with Us!

Text **LOCKDOWN** to 22828 to stay up-to-date with new releases, sneak peaks, contests and more...

Like our page on Facebook:
Lock Down Publications

Join Lock Down Publications/The New Era Reading Group

Visit our website:
www.lockdownpublications.com

Follow us on Instagram:
Lock Down Publications

Email Us: We want to hear from you!

PROLOGUE
January 8, 2023

Every inch of Voltaire's six-foot-four frame was damp with sweat, his rock-hard abs and pectoral muscles glistening with it as he did pull-up after pull-up in the 1,800-square-foot home gym at his half-brother Keondre Muck's thirty-million-dollar Miami Beach mansion.

The Air Pods in his ears were playing *Kut-Throat Bill* Volume 1, Kodak Black's latest album, and his eyes—the cold, dark, nefarious eyes of a domestic terrorist—were trained on Whitney Clarrett, the most beautiful woman he'd ever been lucky enough to call his girlfriend.

She and Bunny, Keondre's girlfriend, were doing sit-ups in front of a mirror halfway across the room, both of them wearing sports bras, yoga pants, and Nike running shoes. Whitney was the thicker of the two, a heartachingly attractive yellow bone with a waterfall of jet-black hair she currently had tied back in a modest ponytail, and she had a big fat ass that made Voltaire's dick jump every time he looked at it.

It was hard to believe that it had been a full six months since Voltaire first laid eyes on thirty-six-year-old Whitney Clarrett. She had flown down from her northwest Indiana hometown to hang out with Bunny on July seventh of last year, and she'd only flown back home a couple of time since, to pack her bags and try convincing her four teenage children to join her in South Beach. Not wanting to switch schools before graduation, Whitney's three daughters—Ava and

Eva, her seventeen-year-old set of identical twins, and fifteen- year-old Joselyn—had opted to stay where they were, and her eighteen-year-old son, Lil' Jimmy, who'd recently gotten an apartment with his girlfriend, Crystal, hadn't even considered leaving.

This was perfect for Voltaire. It meant he could have Whitney all to himself, without the constant bother of having to deal with her children and their juvenile opinions of him. God knew how much he hated dealing with children. He had twelve of them, by eight different women, and all of his children had grown to be just as money-hungry as their mothers.

Not that the money mattered all that much. Voltaire was the head of the Zoe Pounds Mafia, with fifteen drug houses in the Little Haiti and Overtown sections of Miami that brought in between $70,000 and $90,000 every day of the week. He owned seven high-rise condominiums that he rented out through AirBnB, bringing in an additional $50,000 to $60,000 a month, and on top of that he'd paid $2 million for 20% of Whitney's *iKiss Kosmetics* business, which was now on store shelves in Walmart, Target, and also available on Amazon.com. Whitney's first iKiss store was opening tomorrow, and Voltaire had a surprise party planned for her later tonight to celebrate the grand opening.

As he continued doing his pull-ups—"…ninety-two…ninety-three…"—his mind flashed back to the Hoody mess he'd left in Little Haiti last night. He'd learned three weeks ago that Pierre, one of his workers, was stealing from him, but he hadn't known for sure until he had a hidden camera placed inside the stash house located at 184 Northwest 58th Street. He'd had thirty-four kilos of crystal meth and forty-one kilos of cocaine stashed there, and he'd watched the hidden camera's live video feed from his laptop computer while sitting in the back of his blacked-out Cadillac lying a few blocks down from the stash house. At exactly 2:31 a.m., he'd watched Pierre creep into the master bedroom, open one of the duffel bags, and take out a single kilo of cocaine.

Voltaire and four of his fellow Zoe Pound members were standing outside the front door when Pierre opened it to leave, and Voltaire had slammed the blade of his machete right through Pierre's chest and slowly walked him back into the house.

"A bombaclot like you, steal from me?" Voltaire had asked, holding the machete steady as Pierre stumbled backward, his hands grabbing at the blade, his eyes so wide they seemed to be on the verge of popping right out of their sockets.

Voltaire had ripped the machete blade from Pierre's chest, and when he fell, Voltaire stood over him and immediately began to hack at his head. Pierre brought up his arms to fend off the strong blows from the machete, but it was to no avail. His left hand was the first to go, with the sharp blade cutting clean through his forearm four inches above the wrist. The four fingers of his right hand were next to go, with one of the severed digits dropping down into his gaping mouth as he howled in pain. And then Voltaire landed a direct blow to the side of Pierre's tattooed neck. Then another. And another. Until Pierre's dread-locked head separated from his neck and rolled away from his body.

Afterward, Voltaire had snatched the brick of cocaine from inside Pierre's pants and returned it to the duffel bag before heading back home to Whitney. His men knew the protocol. They would clean up the blood, dismember the rest of Pierre's body, and feed the remains to the alligators in a nearby swap, just as they'd done with the last two dead bodies.

Voltaire snapped out of his reverie as Whitney came walking toward him, dabbing sweat from her pretty face with the towel she had draped around the nape of her neck. He dropped from the pull-up bar and landed flat on the soles of his Dior sneakers. He was two hundred and fifty pounds of solid muscle, dark-skinned with thick dreadlocks branching out around his head. His Rolex Sky Dweller wrist watch was flooded with VVS diamonds, and had cost him $150,000. He'd bought it the day after Keondre signed a four-year contract with the Denver Broncos worth $210 million. Keondre had immediately wired Voltaire four million dollars out of the first $50 million. Voltaire had already blown through half of his $4 million before he even met Whitney, and the $2 million he'd invested in her company had essentially emptied his bank account of legitimate funds.

"My kids'll be flying in at around six this afternoon," she said as she made it to him. She tilted her head back, lifting herself up on her tiptoes, her glossy lips pursed for a smooch. Voltaire lowered his head and planted a loud, smacky kiss on her lips. "My sister's coming too," she added. "My family's been riding with me from the very beginning of this whole iKiss journey."

"I'm proud of you. You deserve everything dat comes your way."

Whitney's smile faltered as she took her iPhone from the side pocket of her stretchy white yoga pants. She went to her text messages. "I just got a text from the ex I told you about. The one who cheated me out of two and a half million dollars. Here, read." She thrust her phone at Voltaire's face, so he took it from her hand and read the message:

'*Candace called and told me about your store opening. I wasn't gonna reach out to you, but she talked me into it. I'll be there with my girl to show support, if it's okay with you.*'

Voltaire handed Whitney the phone back, and he gazed off across the weight room, thinking. Whitney stared up at him, expectantly waiting. Meanwhile, at the opposite end of the room, Bunny took advantage of her break from exercising to twerk her big ass in front of the mirror, recording it for her millions of followers. She was a porn actress—not just any porn actress, but the hottest black porn star of the moment, particularly due to the worldwide fame of her phenomenal blowjob videos—and she had droves of avid fans across every social media platform.

"Yes," Voltaire said finally. "Let him come."

"It'll be good for business, if nothing else," Whitney said, attempting to turn lemons into lemonade. "His girlfriend has ten times as many followers as Bunny on IG. If she posts about my shop, it'll get huge results."

"You'll succeed. No worries. I just want have a chat with the ex-boy. See if we can't get dat two-point-five into your hands before he leaves."

Whitney's beaming smile returned. She rose up on tiptoe again, and this time she added a bit of tongue to her kiss. As she turned and sauntered back across the room, Voltaire envisioned his encounter with Markio Earl going wrong, imagining himself swinging his machete at the ex-boy's neck right in the middle of Biscayne Boulevard. Voltaire would give Markio an ultimatum: either give Whitney the 2.5 million, or face the deadly consequences.

Little did Voltaire know, Markio Earl was a deadly man himself.

Chapter 1

Markio's 7-Eleven gas station cup was filled with ice, Sprite soda, and four ounces of Wockhardt promethazine with codeine syrup. He'd stuffed the blunt he was smoking with eight grams of Black Cherry Gelato. He'd popped two Roxycodone pills to help him relax even more, if that was even possible. It was January eighth, the second Sunday of 2023, and Markio Earl felt more relaxed than ever before.

Although Markio had made a few million dollars selling hundreds of pounds of the same exotic marijuana he was smoking, his passion was writing, which was what he was doing now as he sat in the backseat of the snow-white Rolls-Royce Cullinan his girlfriend had bought him for Christmas. He was on his laptop, typing the final chapters to "The Bird Man 5: The Last Shipment." He'd gotten the other four novels in the series published over the past six months, and all of them were currently on Amazon's bestsellers list in the *African American Fiction* genre. The royalties were nothing compared to the money he made off selling pounds of high-grade marijuana. He'd paid $2 million for two thousand pounds of Black Cherry Gelato back in September, and had already off loaded 1,600 pounds of that at $4,500-a-pound, but fiction writing was his only legitimate source of income, and he was great at doing it, so he went at it relentlessly, writing at all hours of the day and night.

So far, he'd sold more than four hundred thousand $4.99 ebooks and a hundred thousand $14.99 paperback books, bringing in more than $950,000 in royalties, and that was after his publisher at Lockup Publications and all the distributors got their cut. The taxes were a bitch, but so what? Markio was up. He had more than $9 million in drug money stashed away, and his girlfriend Nikkia's net worth was $241 million. Together, they were a quarter-billion-dollar couple, and if the past six months were any sign of what was to come, things were only going to get better.

Markio took a break from typing and sat back in his comfortable, heated, white leather seat. Sipping from his cup of Lean, he blew twin streams of weed smoke out his nose and tipped his head back against the headrest. He was short, light-skinned, and handsome, a 35-year-old member of the Traveling Vice Lords with neat little waves in his low-cut hair, and two teardrops inked under his left eye. The teardrops represented two homicides he'd committed over the decades ago; if he had teardrops for every murder he'd ever committed, he'd be crying a river. Six months ago, he and his guys had gone on a two-day killing spree that ultimately left ten bodies across Michigan City, Indiana and the West side of Chicago, Illinois. He'd done three of those murders himself, and for the rest he'd paid tens of thousands of dollars, not letting up until every one of his opps were dead and gone.

Markio looked out his rear passenger's side window at a nearly toothless drug addict in a dingy brown hoodie and threadbare jeans. The old man was standing on the snow-covered sidewalk in front of 1520 South Homan Avenue, his warm breaths making smoke in the twenty-eight-degree air as he stared down at his handful of change, using one finger to stir around the quarters and dimes and nickels, as if he'd find a hundred-dollar bill hidden somewhere beneath the pile of coins. The woman standing beside him had been wise enough to put on a coat, a filthy burgundy one that went way down to her ancient leather boars. She had her hands cupped together in front of her mouth, and was leaning in over the man's handful of coins, examining them while blowing hot air into her freezing palms. They made a decision and started off down Homan, and Markio searched the street for something else to inspire his writing.

That was how he spotted the backed-out Grand Cherokee Trackhawk Jeep as it turned off of 16th Street and came trundling slowly in his direction. He sat forward, knitting his brow and reaching for the micro Draco pistol that lay on the seat next to him, its 70-round drum fully loaded. He could see that the two young black men in the front seats of the Jeep were eyeing his gaudy white Rolls-Royce SUV. Then, their attention shifted to the bone-white Range Rover parked in front of him, just as Markio's cousins—Kay and Buck— came walking out of 1520 South Homan Avenue, wheeling their Louis Vuitton suitcases behind them.

The Jeep rolled on past as Kay popped open the Range Rover's rear storage compartment and loaded in the two suitcases. He and Buck were flying down to Miami with Markio and Nikkia, on Nikkia's Gulfstream 550 private jet, but the trip was the furthest thing from Markio's mind as he twisted around in his seat, keeping an eye on the Trackhawk as it continued on to the next street and made a right turn, vanishing down Douglas Boulevard.

Markio tapped the driver's seat, waking up his 29-year-old sister, Shakia, whom he'd hired to be his driver four months ago. Then he lowered his window and shouted for Buck to come over to his door. Years of gangbanging on Chicago's west side streets had made Buck much more vigilant than the average man. Before Markio could even open his mouth to speak, Buck opened his black leather Louis Vuitton jacket and showed his Glock 23 with the 30 shot clip sticking out of it.

"That was Worm's son—Binky, and his lil' guy, Jack, in the Trackhawk," he said when he got to Markio's door. "You know your nephew whacked Lil' Worm and Mannie the same night Big Worm got whacked. That lil' nigga Binky been actin' like he got a problem about it. He gon' fuck around and join his daddy."

Markio was shaking his head. "Nah, fuck that. We gon' get the matter taken care of right now. Come on, y'all follow me. Shakia, bust a U and slide down Douglas."

"Hold on, Lord," Buck said, and Markio could almost sense what was coming next. "You can't be movin' like you used to move. You got a bag now, lil' cuz. You a bestsellin' author, ridin' around in a fuckin' Rolls Royce truck. You too fuckin' rich to be shootin' at these hoe-ass niggas We got lil' homies for shit like this. Drop a bag on them niggas and let the wolves eat."

Markio had nothing more to say. He raised his window and took one last pull on his blunt before he passed it forward to his youngest sister, ignoring the discontented look on Buck's brown-hued face as he walked back to his Range Rover and got in with his brother—Kay. Setting his cup of Lean in the cup holder, Markio closed his MacBook Pro and picked up his Draco. Shakia started the Cullinan and made a U-turn in the middle of Homan Avenue, and Buck was right behind them in the Range Rover.

Markio had no gloves or masks available to him at the moment, and he was fine with that. He'd killed men bare-faced before, though never while dressed as richly as he was now. The four-diamond tennis chains hanging around his neck were worth almost $200,000, and Nikkia had paid $340,000 for the icy Patek Philippe watch he wore on his left wrist. His white Christian Dior leather jacket had cost him twenty grand, and the rest of his all-white outfit—skull cap, sweater, T-shirt, sweat pants, and sneakers—were also by Dior. He had $100,000 in bank-new hundreds crammed down into the deep pockets of his sweats, and another $400,000 in the Louis Vuitton duffel bag behind his seat. But none of that mattered. If someone was going to "act like" they wanted Markio or one of his family members dead, he would get them first, no matter how much money he had when the pump-fake occurred.

There was a stretch of black ice at the corner of Homan and Douglas; the Cullinan glided across it as Shakia attempted to make the turn, but she was able to steer into it and brake. Markio hardly even noticed the slide. His eyes were on the black Jeep parked several blocks down, in front of an apartment building on the opposite side of the boulevard. The passenger's door was open, and there was someone standing there next to it, but the Jeep was parked near the end of the boulevard, too far away to discern any clear details.

Markio pointed at it. "That black Jeep down there. Go all the way down to the end of Douglas and turn left onto Albany. You can park there, and I'll walk around the corner."

Shakia only nodded. Not only did she look a lot like Markio, she also acted a lot like him, with a temper as short as a baby midget on his knees. She'd beat up a bunch of bitches, and Markio had shot up a bunch of niggas. They were as much alike that the family had begun to call her his twin.

Markio's iPhone rang with a FaceTime call from Nikkia. He looked from his phone to his Draco and hesitated; he'd never ignored a call from Nikkia, but right now there was so much adrenaline coursing through him that he almost did it. But he didn't. He answered the video call, and Nikkia's wetly-glossed lips formed an amorous smile as Markio removed his Dior sunglasses to show her his bloodshot brown eyes.

"What up, baby?" he said, glancing from his phone screen to the road ahead. There was still a good three blocks to go, and with all the snow slickening the street, it would be slow going.

"Damiko and Leon are finishing up packing now," said Nikkia, speaking of two of her teenage sons. Her third teen boy, Darious, was away at Indiana State University, studying to become a computer engineer. "We should be ready to go in a couple of minutes. I packed you some more shorts and T-shirts. It'll be eighty-eight degrees in Miami tomorrow, and ninety degrees when we land."

"Okay," Markio said with a nod. "I'm headed to the airport now. Just gotta make one quick stop."

"Are your cousins still coming?"

"Yeah. We just left from in front of Buck's house a minute ago. I sat outside writing while they packed. Got about three more chapters to write and I'll be done with the next book in the Bird Man series. You can be whoever you wanna be in my movie. Shit, you can be one of the main characters, if that's what you wanna do." Markio picked up his cup and took another sip of his narcotic beverage before placing it back in the cup-holder. "Let me call you right back. I gotta make a quick stop."

"It's not like the stop you made back in July, is it?" Nikkia asked, her eyes squinted accusingly.

Markio chuckled at the question. She was talking about the night he'd shot Big Worm in the face while she was on the phone listening. "Nah, baby. I told you, those days are over for me. I'll be thirty-six years old in a couple of weeks. I'm focused on my writing career. That's it, that's all."

"Mm-hm," she hummed skeptically. "Well, hurry up. We'll be at Midway in about an hour."

"Stop and grab me some Flamin' that's on the way. I'll meet y'all there."

Markio blew his beautiful brown-skinned queen a kiss and then ended the video call, picking up his Draco and staring ahead between the front seats. The Draco was a fully automatic weapon, just like the twin Glock model 23 he had in the shoulder holster inside his designer jacket; one could never be too careful in the savage streets of Chicago.

His heart was a little drummer boy in his chest, beating out an erratic drumline as his five-hundred-thousand-dollar luxury SUV rumbled down Douglas Boulevard. It didn't help that no less than ten people raised their smartphones to capture videos of the passing Rolls Royce Cullinan. If any of them still had their cameras trained on his truck just a few moments from now, he knew the footage would likely be used as Exhibit A in a future criminal trial.

As Shakia passed Kedzie Avenue, puffing the thick blunt and steering the truck like she owned it, Markio was able to get a better look at the Jeep that was now parked just one city block ahead of him. The guy from the passenger seat of the Trackhawk was standing out on the sidewalk, talking to Tammy—a cute young thot who'd been blowing up Markio's Instagram direct messages for a couple of months now. It looked like they were exchanging information, both of them looking down at their smart phones as they carried on a conversation.

The hawk-eyed driver wasn't looking. Markio was looking at him, and he was looking at Markio's truck. There was a light snow fall coming down, sprinkling the windshield with tiny flakes. A burst of wind plowed into the Cullinan, rocking it a little, but Markio stayed focused on the Trackhawk.

"He's lookin' right at us," Shakia noted. "We're in the middle of the trenches in a fuckin' Rolls Royce truck, stickin' out like a sore thumb. We should've jumped in a steamer. A Honda or a Nissan or some'n. Anything but this big dumb Rolls Royce."

"Just pull around the side of that building."

Markio's mind was made up, and there was no talking him out of Binky's uncle—Bam—a millionaire heroin dealer and 5 Star Universal Elite for the Travelers (and also the only other man from the neighborhood with a Rolls Royce truck). Bam was like family to Markio, and he hated to be responsible for another member of Bam's family being put in the ground, especially when everyone already suspected him of killing Big Worm, but he'd rather it be them in a casket than him.

As Shakia braked at the east end of the boulevard and turned north onto Albany, the Trackhawk driver's door swung open and Binky stepped out, his eyes glued to the two white SUV's. He was a big boy, about 6'3" and close to three hundred pounds, wearing a blue leather Pelle Pelle jacket and fitted designer jeans. He yelled something to his ultra-thin partner, Jock, who immediately turned away from Tammy to look at Markio's truck, just as Buck pulled his Range Rover to an abrupt sliding stop and bailed out with his Glock in hand. Kay jumped out at the same time, aiming a Glock with a 50-shot drum magazine. Both guns had steel switches that made them fire on fully-automatic, and as they opened fire on Binky, the rapid *BRRRRR* of gunfire thundered across the land.

Binky whipped out his pistol a second before a spray of bullets stitched across his rotund belly, knocking him back against his open door and shattering the window behind him. Jock took off running into the apartment building, and Tammy smartly dropped flat to the snow-laden sidewalk as fifteen or twenty more bullets pounded into Binky's chest and face. It all happened too quickly for Markio to react. He only caught a few seconds of the action before Shakia sped off down Albany and seconds later they were soaring down Roosevelt Road, Markio still clutching his Draco as Buck's Range Rover veered around the Cullinan and raced ahead.

"Bitch!" Markio exclaimed heatedly. "I ain't even get a shot off."

Shakia glanced at him in the rearview mirror. It was an *Are-you-serious?* look, and Markio said nothing because he was serious. As serious as a heart attack. Markio Earl was the kind of gansgta who'd murder you over a joke, so his approach to threats against him and his family went without saying. He was glad that Binky was stretched out in the street with at least thirty bullet holes in his body, and genuinely pissed that he hadn't been able to join in on the action, and he was more than ready for whatever repercussions came because of it.

***

There were eight young gang members at each of Bam's five drug spots: five for security, one to deal the drugs, one to collect the money, and one to oversee the operation. Bam had blessed the overseers with the rank of 5-Star Branch Elite, and they took their jobs seriously, sometimes issuing physical violations to habitual law-breakers. They worked eight-hour shifts, from 6:00 a.m. to 2:00 p.m., and from 3:00 p.m. to 11:00 p.m. Bam knew better than to keep his trap house open all night. The night shift was too dangerous, not just from potential robbers but also from opposing gang members who used the cover of night to slide on their opps with little risk of detection. Bam supplied each trap spot with two assault rifles and three handguns, and his young bulls used them quite often.

Leroy "Bam" Patterson Jr. leased a $5,000-a-month Wrigleyville town house worth $4.4 million. He and his girlfriend—Malaysia—were there, running yesterday's piles of cash through two electronic money counters on the dining room table and rubber-banding the cash after the machines spit out the bills, when he got the phone call from Jock.

"Binky just got hit up," Jock said, his voice shaky with panic. "Not even two minutes ago. Twelve ain't even pulled up yet. Had just stepped out of his truck when Markio and his people drew down on him. They had switches on them guns, man. Lil' bra didn't stand a chance. I had my pipe on me, but I ain't got no switch. They would've whacked me too. I had to get low."

A heavy weight of grief fell upon Bam's lungs when Jock revealed that Binky had been shot down. Bam released his grip on a handful of twenty-dollar bills and let them free fall to the mahogany floorboards all around his white Amiri flip-flops. Malaysia had been feeding another pile of hundreds into the money counter, and she stopped to look at Bam, her pretty hazel eyes replete with concern. She was an exotic dancer contracted exclusively to Redbone's Gentleman's Club, which made it easy for her to deposit all the one and five dollar bills Bam made from drug dealing into her bank account without having to answer any questions.

"What's wrong, Bam?" Malaysia asked. Her four-inch Bottega heels clicked on the glassy hardwood floor as she stepped close to him. "What happened this time?"

Bam spoke into his AirPods, "You sure he dead?"

Jock said, "I'm walkin' back out there now, but I think he is. I'm almost sure he is. It was too many shots. Ain't no way he survived that shit."

Bam was grinding his teeth together. The grief was quickly morphing into anger. He'd suspected Markio of killing his brother, Big Worm, but he hadn't known for sure, so he'd let it go. He'd known that Markio's nephew Tyquan had killed Lil' Worm that same night, but that was only because Big Worm had sent Lil' Worm and his boys to rob the house Tyquan lived in, so he'd let that go, too. He'd paid for both funerals and grieved with his loved ones and promised to get even with whoever had killed his brother, but in the six months since Big Worm's murder, no one had come forward with any information about his shooter, even after Bam had offered $250,000.

But this was different. Jock claimed to have witnessed the shooting and knew it was Markio and his people. If that was the case, Bam had no choice but to declare a war against one of his own. And a war against Markio Earl was a war against the entire Earl Family, a multi-million-dollar conglomerate that included two well-known street millionaires: Markio, who'd gotten on with five million dollars of Big Worm's money, was now one of the biggest exotic weed connects in Chicago; and his younger cousin—Bankroll Reese—owned Redbone's and a dozen other successful strip clubs across seven states. Bam had no idea how much money Markio had to his name, but he knew that Markio's girlfriend was worth a few hundred million, and according to celebritynetworth.com Bankroll Reese was worth $58 million. Altogether, Bam had a little over $12 million in drug money, stashed away in five different locations, and the concert-promoting business he'd started to launder his drug money was now worth $2.3 million. The only real advantage Bam had over the Earls was his power over the mob. He was one of the highest ranking TVLs on the west side of Chicago, the chief of the Travelers in North Lawndale, and he had a few hundred heartless young shooters under him who wouldn't hesitate to do whatever he asked. Sure, some of them would side with Markio and his family, but Bam could handle them.

If what Jock had just told him was true, Bam was going to put $250,000 on Markio's head.

There weren't many men who would turn down that kind of money.

Bam could hear the wind blowing from Jock's end of the line. It was a cold, snowy morning, though nowhere near as frigid as it had been over the Christmas weekend.

"Damn, big homie," Jock said in a weak, defeated tone. "Yeah, he over with, man. They did him bad. He got hit a few times in the face, in the neck, in the chest, a bunch of times in the stomach. Shit. I'm about to take a picture and send it to you."

"You sure it was Markio who did it?"

"I didn't see him at all, but it was definitely him and his people. Markio is the only nigga with a white Rolls Royce truck, and that was Buck's white Range Rover behind it. The shooters jumped out the Range Rover. I didn't get to see who was shootin', but we had just rode past Buck's crib and saw him and Kay gettin' in the Range Rover. Binky was talkin' about slidin' on Markio about Big Worm and Lil' Worm getting' killed, so we drove past there, and I guess they saw us lookin'."

19

Bam was far too upset to say anything else, so he ended the call and looked at the picture Jock had just sent. He cringed. Binky's face was a bloody mess. There were two clear holes in his forehead, one through the side of his fat nose, another just below his left eye. One bullet had torn through his top lip and shattered a lateral incisor. He was propped up against the open driver door, his head tilted back against the bullet-riddled door panel, his pants soaked from the slush he was sitting in, and the blood pouring from his many wounds.

Malaysia looked at Bam's phone screen and gasped. "You said Markio did that?"

Bam had to take a seat, plopping down in one of the leather-upholstered dining chairs. He was 6'3.5" and weighed exactly 254 pounds, a bald dark-skinned man in his early forties who dressed like a rich gangsta rapper, never leaving the house without at least three diamond-encrusted Cuban-link necklaces twinkling around his neck and a quarter-million-dollar watch glistening on his wrist. He wore a diamond Audemars watch today, and two of the three diamond pendants hanging from his necklaces read *Fin Ball Promo*, with a five-ball and pool stick beneath the words. It was the logo for Fin Ball Promotions, his concert-promoting business. The third pendant was huge and simply read *BAM* in diamond lettering.

"If this nigga just had my nephew killed," Bam said, unable to take his eyes off the sickening image on his iPhone screen, "he ain't gon' live to see the sunset."

"Oh, Jesus." Malaysia pressed the manicured fingers of one hand flat against the chest of her black Versace robe. "Not Markio. I thought you said he was like a brother to you?"

Bam lowered his head as the tears began to fall, pattering down onto the floor between his feet. He hardly even noticed Malaysia taking the phone from his hand. She pushed him back in the chair and sat sideways across the lap of his red

Amiri sweatpants, cradling his head against her buxom chest and rubbing his bald scalp.

Over the loss of his nephew, Bam cried tears of anger and grief. His rage at Markio and the pain the lingering image of Binky's dead body brought to his heart combined to create a fiery thirst for revenge. He would give himself a moment to calm down, to regain control of his emotions, and then he'd make his move.

Chapter 2

The Federal investigation into Markio Earl and the Traveling Vice Lords officially began on July 7th, 2022, when the MCPD and the ATF had failed to gather enough evidence to charge Markio in the slew of murders that took place over a 48-hour period in Michigan City, Indiana. A federal informant entrusted with the task of getting Markio to admit to his involvement in the murders was supposed to meet up with him that night at The Visionary Lounge, a popular night club on Chicago's west side, but the informant was gunned down half a block away from the club in what federal authorities believed was a planned hit orchestrated by Markio and his gang.

In Michigan City, the local police had arrested Swayson and Shannon Swanson, the two brothers they suspected Markio had paid to commit at least four of the murders. There was a warrant out for Brandon Arnold, a transsexual the police believed had set up one of the murder victims, but he'd fled the city shortly after the murder and hadn't been seen or heard from since. The world-renowned Bostic and Staples law firm, of which Markio's girlfriend—Nikkia Staples—was a founding partner, had picked up the Swanson brothers' cases. Shannon Swanson was already back on the streets, found not guilty after a fast and speedy jury trial, and Swayson was only in prison because he'd been arrested with a bottle of ecstasy pills in his pocket, violating his probation; he too had been found not guilty in the fast and speedy trial.

When a hidden audio recorder led police to the motive behind the spate of shootings—that Markio had purchased a locker at a storage auction and ended up with five million dollars of some Chicago drug kingpin's money—a separate federal investigation was launched against Herman Patterson, the Chicago man whose name the storage locker had been registered in. But when the FBI arrived to stake out Herman Patterson's only known address, a basement apartment on the west side of Chicago, they'd found it blocked off with yellow crime scene tape and surrounded by CPD patrol cars. Herman Patterson had been found with a single gunshot wound to the head just minutes after the informant was gunned down near The Visionary Lounge. Patterson's eighteen-year-old son and one of his friends were killed the same night, shot down as they attempted to enter Markio's mother's home in Michigan City.

The FBI hadn't uncovered much in the six months since the deadly night in July. Markio seemed to be on the straight and narrow. A federal judge had signed an order authorizing the monitoring of Markio's cell phone, and there was a team of FBI agents watching his every move, but so far they'd found nothing. His text messages were mostly to his family members and close friends, and none of them ever mentioned anything criminal. His FaceTime calls with Nikkia Staples were the typical conversations you'd expect from legitimate lovers. He looked intoxicated in a lot of the videos, but recreational marijuana use was legal in Illinois, and Staples had gotten Markio released from parole a year early back in October, so there was no foul there. Markio may have been involved with the unsolved July murders, but there was no proof, and the only thing he did nowadays was publish his novels and promote them at book signings all across the country.

In fact, FBI Special Agent Jacob Walloby was seconds away from pulling the plug on the entire investigation when the two undercover agents he'd had trailing Markio for the past couple of weeks phoned him in his office.

"There's been a shooting," said Agent Deborah Wade. "Well, actually a murder. Some guy just got shot to pieces outside of his Jeep on Douglas Boulevard. There was a white Range Rover following behind Markio's Rolls Royce when the Range Rover suddenly stopped and two guys jumped out shooting. We were about two blocks behind the action, so we couldn't really get a good look at the shooters, but they definitely jumped out of the Range Rover."

Walloby was out of his seat, pacing his office floor, a burgeoning smirk lifting one side of his thin-lipped mouth. "Please tell me you got all this on video."

"No, I'm sorry. No video of the shooting. Like I said, we were two blocks away, and I didn't have the long range lens set up on my camera."

"What about that Range Rover? Did you get the plates?"

"That's another negative. I was watching through my binoculars, and Pierce was driving. We tried chasing after them but they were long gone by the time we made it to the actual shooting scene. We did watch two men walk out of a house on Homan Avenue and load two suitcases into the Range Rover while Markio sat parked in his Rolls Royce. One of the guys had a brown complexion, about my color, and the other guy was very light in complexion, maybe a shade or two lighter than Markio."

"I'll have Levy access the traffic cameras from the North Lawndale area, see if we can spot that Range Rover," Walloby said, opening his office door and looking out at all the in-house agents, seated at the desks in their cubicles.

"One more thing," said Wade. "I ran the plates on the Jeep at the crime scene. Comes back to Bernard Patterson. Wanna take a wild swing at who his father was?"

"Herman Patterson. Big Worm." Walloby's smirk grew into a full-on smile.

"You got it. Markio's nephew—Tyquan Holton—killed "Little Worm" in self-defense six months ago. Big Worm was killed that same night, and now another of his sons has been murdered by a member of Markio's entourage."

Walloby spotted Steve Levy, his computer investigations expert, walking in with a tray of Starbucks coffees and waved him over. "Good job, Wade," he said, walking back to his desk. "Go back and get the address to the house those two shooters walked out of and then come back to the office. I have a plan."

He put down his smart phone and turned to his computer to pull up the FBI file on Markio Earl. Compiled over the past six months, the file contained every known detail of Markio's life, from his extensive juvenile record to his alleged ties to multiple criminal street gangs, including the Traveling Vice Lords (of which he was a reputed member), the Unknown Vice Lords, the Conservative Vice Lords, the Mafia Insane Vice Lords, the Black P. Stones, and the Four Corner Hustlers. There were reports of Markio being named the suspect in numerous shooting investigations. There were photos of his gang tattoos—a big ALMIGHTY across the top of his back and a Louis Vuitton sign on the front of his left leg that symbolized his allegiance to the Vice Lords—and crime scene photos from the ten homicides he was suspected of either committing himself or having committed on his behalf, including the homicide for which he'd served fifteen years in the Indiana Department of Corrections. Surveillance photos from prison showed him mingling with other known gang members, beating and stabbing inmates who'd offended him in one way or another, and even assaulting several prison guards.

But the thing that interested Walloby most was the timeline of photos and videos that had been captured over the past six months, particularly the photos an undercover FBI agent had taken at last week's New Year's Day NFL game between the Chicago Bears and the Detroit Lions. He clicked on one of the photos and was zooming in on the faces of the men in Markio's entourage when Steve Levy entered his office after having doled out two of the coffees from his beverage tray.

In the photo, Markio Earl could be seen in the skybox with Nikkia Staples and ten others that arrived with them in two identical Mercedes Benz Sprinter vans. One of the men was very light in complexion, almost mulatto, and he was seated next to a taller, slimmer man whose brown complexion was about the same as Agent Wade's.

"Here you go. John Wayne style: no sugar, no cream," Levy said, placing Walloby's coffee on the desk. "I don't know how you can stomach your coffee that way. I'd die if mine didn't have at least four sugar twins in it. I can do without creamer, but sugar twins are an absolute must-have."

"Real men drink their coffee like they do their whiskey: straight, with no cut on it," Walloby proclaimed, closing one age-spotted hand around his cup and bringing it to his mouth for a refreshing sip. He was sixty-six years old and had been with the bureau since he was twenty-three years young, back when heroin had ravaged the country and crack—cocaine— was unheard of. He motioned toward his computer screen, and Agent Levy—a broad-shouldered bulk of a man with an uneven crew cut and arms the size of *The Rock*'s—stepped around the desk to get a look at the photo Walloby was studying.

"I thought you said you were done with the whole Markio Earl thing? Levy said. "The guy's clean. He's an author. We can't lock him up for writing books."

"I was done with the Markio Earl investigation. That was before Agent Wade called me a few minutes ago saying she'd just watched two of Markio's associates jump out of a white Range Rover and gun down some kid on Douglas Boulevard." Walloby pointed a thick-nailed fore finger at the two men he'd been eyeing in the photo. "I believe it was them. The other guys in this picture rotate in and out of

Markio's inner circle, but these two are almost always with him."

"And they haven't been arrested?"

"Nope. Wade only saw them through her binoculars, and they sped off before she and Pierce could get to them. We're not gonna make the arrest anyway. That's on the CPD. I just need you to go through the traffic cams and see if you can get the plates on that Range Rover." Another short sip of scalding-hot coffee, and Walloby added, "The kid they killed was another one of Herman Patterson's sons. Herman—the dead guy Markio supposedly got the five million dollars from."

"Oh, yeah." Levy nodded. His big pink face was red from the cold he'd endured walking through the parking lot, his nose a bit runny. He sniffled and drank from his coffee, which was undoubtedly as light-colored as Markio's close associates. "Emerson just opened a RICO investigation on Herman's brother not even a week ago. They call him Bam. He's the top guy for the TVLs in Holy City, drives a Rolls-Royce truck just like Markio's, only his is black. In fact, he and Markio grew up together on 15th and Trumbull. Emerson's working with the DEA on the case. They believe Bam may be the head of a large-scale heroin distribution network."

Walloby became thoughtfully silent, steepling his hands in front of his chin. If Bam was Herman Patterson's brother, and also the leader of a violent criminal street gang, then Markio Earl had likely just landed himself in a world of trouble by knocking off one of Bam's nephews.

"You know what?" Walloby said, after a time. "It may be best to take the same hands of approach as we did with that south side gangster rapper. What was his name again?"

"Lil Durk." Levy said it distastefully. "I still say we should indict that fucker."

"No, no. Wrong approach. Taxpayer dollars would be wasted going through the whole arrest process, then the court proceeding, and guys like him can hire one high-priced attorney good enough to suppress critical evidence and beat the case at trial. But see," Walloby said, turning to study the sky box photo again, "when you know they're at war with opposing street gangs or, in this case, opposing members of the same street gang, it's always cheaper and easier to give them the space and time to slaughter each other."

Levy nodded his huge head and sniffled. "I guess I see your point."

"Of course you do. Bam's a gang leader, so he's likely in possession of all kinds of weapons. Whether or not Markio actually recovered five million dollars from Herman Patterson's storage locker, he's a known gang member with a popular book series and a wealthy, famous girlfriend. I guarantee you he's already supplied his people with dozens of firearms. Let's wait and see how all this plays out. We may not even need to build a case against Markio. This guy, Bam, will take him off the streets long before we could ever hope to get a pair of handcuffs on him."

Levy was nodding again; Walloby was nodding too, proud to see that one of his toughest protégés was finally seeing the bigger picture. An hour later, Walloby called a meeting with the agents he'd had listening in on Markio Earl's phone calls and tracking his every move over the past six months. Several of them—especially Wade and Pierce, who'd been dressed up as a drug-addicted couple, standing out in the cold next to Markio's Rolls Royce just over an hour ago—were shocked to hear that they were ending the investigation into a man suspected of being responsible for at least ten homicides. But Levy didn't say a word. Levy understood the method to Walloby's madness.

Markio Earl was much better off in a grave than in Federal custody.

Chapter 3

Tucked away at the end of a cul-de-sac in the wealthy Chicago suburb of Burr Ridge, Nikkia Staples' massive 11,750-square-foot gray-stone mansion stood like a behemoth Disney castle on twelve acres of land that included a lake, heated horse stables for her three English stallions, and a huge backyard swimming pool with a grotto, a Jacuzzi, and a twenty-foot water slide.

There were eight bedrooms and ten bathrooms inside the mansion, as well as ten fireplaces, three kitchens, a two-story walk-in closet in the master bedroom suite, and a forty-seat theater. The overhead included a personal chef, three full-time maids, a horse caregiver, and round-the-clock armed security. The guards patrolled the perimeter of the house like Secret Service agents, in black suits and dark sunglasses, with mics in their ears and pistols on their hips. They rumbled across the vast estate in golf carts, and sometimes on all-terrain vehicles, always on the watch for intruders.

Markio loved the place, but he wasn't feeling particularly joyous at the moment.

"Why not?" Nikkia asked, pressing the knuckles of her clenched fists into her hips and glowering at him. "Why in the hell not?"

They were in the east wing kitchen, Nikkia scowling down at him as he sat eating an overstuffed chicken burrito and perusing text messages on his second smart phone, a prepaid iPhone he used to conduct his business in the streets.

He had just told Nikkia that he no longer wanted to travel to Miami, and she wasn't exactly happy about it.

"Some bullshit just went down out west," he said. "I can't leave the city right now. Gotta take care of some'n in the streets first. I'll fly down there tomorrow."

Nikkia was bundled up in a white leather Chanel coat with a plush fur lining. A thick Chanel scarf was wrapped around her neck, and a matching skullcap was pulled down over her ears. In the famous words of John Legend, she was *ready to go right now*, as were her two teenage boys, but Markio wasn't ready to go anywhere.

"You cannot be serious," Nikkia muttered incredulously. "I made plans for us. I'm being paid a lot of money just to make an appearance at Club LIV. They comped us a table, free bottles. A couple of my friends are gonna be there–and not just any friends, I mean famous friends. You now Kash Doll? That's my girl. She'll be there. Lakeyah will be there. Cardi B and Offset are supposed to be there. Oh, and how could I forget? Alexis will be there, too, so you know…"

Nikkia went on speaking, but Markio's mind was stuck on the last celebrity name she'd mentioned. Alexus. As in the Alexus. Alexus Castilla, Queen A—the wealthiest bad bitch on the planet. Alexus's net worth was in the hundreds of billions. She was the gorgeous Black and Mexican woman that everyone believed was a member of Mexico's reigning drug cartel, and her husband was the infamous Blake "Bullet Face" King, the only Grammy winning rap artist who was richer than Jay-Z and more gangster than EST Gee. Bullet Face was originally from Michigan City, Indiana, but he'd spent a lot of time in Chicago with the Vice Lords in Markio's old neighborhood. All of that had happened while Markio was away in prison, but everyone had told him about what life was like when Alexus and Blake were around— thousands of kilos of cocaine, millions upon millions of dollars in drug money flowing through the hood, Bugattis, Ferraris, and Lamborghinis racing up and down 16th Street.

Alexus Castilla was about as famous as Beyonce, her body as curvaceous as Lela Anthony's.

The possibility of meeting Alexus in person changed Markio's mind in an instant.

"Alright, baby," he said, looking up at Nikkia's scorching-hot stare. "I'll go. Just give me a minute to make a couple of calls. I'll meet you out in the truck."

"We're taking the Sprinter," Nikkia said, and stormed out of the kitchen, followed by her nerdy Nigerian assistant—Zia, who'd been standing out in the hallway, replying to emails on her iPhone.

Markio grinned and chuckled at his lady's fiery attitude. She was a bad bitch, too, and famous in her own right. She'd gotten a few nips and tucks to make her body as curvy and flawless as Alexus's. She and Markio were about the same height, and she'd spent a few million dollars on his wardrobe and jewelry to make sure he matched her fly. Their walk-in closets were a fashion lover's paradise. Their six-car garage held two black Mercedes Sprinter vans and four white Rolls Royces—a Phantom, a Wraith, and two Cullinans.

On his trap phone, Markio read three new text messages. The first was from Andre "Crasher" Cowherd, a Gangster Disciple from the south side of Chicago who'd been so much a factor in his Englewood neighborhood that they'd nicknamed his area Crashville. Markio had sold him a hundred pounds of exotic weed for $420,000, and Crasher sold every pound for $6,000 each the first day he received the load. His text read, 'Lord I need anutha 100."

Another text was from the King Squad Twins, a pair of identical twin brothers who were originally from Harvey, Illinois but resided in Indianapolis. They'd taken three hundred pounds off Markio's hands, and new King Squad Tae wanted to know if Markio had any pints of Wockhardt for sale.

The third text was the one that essentially poured every ounce of blood from Markio's body into a pot and placed it on a stove with the burner on high. Soon, it was boiling, and Markio was clenching his teeth, his nostrils flaring like a wolf on the hunt.

The text message was from Bam, and it simply read: 'ALL THE WAY UP!'

Markio understood the threat. It was up and it was stuck there. He was not at war with the leader of his own gang, and though he knew that a lot of the Lords would ultimately side with him, most of them would undoubtedly take Bam's word as law.

But Markio was prepared. He'd spent more than a hundred thousand dollars on guns and ammunition. He had Mac-10s, Mac-11s, Kel-Tecs, Glocks, Rugers, AR pistols, and Dracos, and every gun had at least one high-capacity magazine. He had a bullet-proof vest, which he had on now, and the great thing about Nikkia owning a private jet was that he could drive right up to the airplane with his personal guns stashed in his duffel bag.

Maybe a trip to Miami Beach was exactly what he needed. He had money, and he had a small army of die-hard gang members on his team. During his fifteen-year stint in the Indiana prison system, he'd gown close to Vice Lords from multiple other branches, including Maria Insane Vice Lords, Unknown Vice Lords, Undertaker Vice Lords, and Conservative Vice Lords. He'd earned the respect of the Black Disciples and the Gangster Disciples, Black P. Stones like the King Squad Twins, and 4 Corner Hustlers like Big Wayne and Q, and many of them would spin for him free of charge. Not to mention his own Travelers, and all the other gang members he'd met over the years. Those connections were the reason he'd been able to get rid of sixteen hundred pounds of weed in a matter of months. He even had some white Aryan Brotherhood members who would kill for him if he made the call.

Frankly, Markio had too many mob ties and too many millions to be concerned about a war. He'd put $250,000 on

Bam's head and relax in Miami Beach while his shooters tracked Bam down and knocked him off. It would be a piece of cake, he thought.

And the thought could not have been further from the truth.

***

"You're way cooler than our dad," Mike said, pushing his Beats headphones down around his slender brown neck. "He's a lame. He thinks smoking weed is bad. He doesn't let us listen to rap music. He's never been in the streets, never met a real gang member like you in his life. One time, a guy snatched our mom's purse, and he didn't even chase after the guy. Just dialed nine-one-one. We're so glad our mom met you. You're the coolest stepdad ever. We know you'll protect Mom."

Markio chuckled at the kid, even as Nikkia turned in her seat and gave her son a look. Mike was seventeen, a video game fanatic who was always itching for an ass-whooping in *Black Ops: Modern Warfare II*. His brother—Leon—was sixteen, and as usual he was seated quietly beside Mike, texting his new girlfriend as the pilots eased Nikkia's forty-million-dollar Gulfstream V out of the private airplane hanger at Midway International Airport.

Buck and Kay were seated across the aisle from Markio and Nikkia, their eyes red-veined and asquint from the three blunts they'd smoked on the way to the airport. They had left Buck's Range Rover in the long-term parking section, where it would stay until Buck traded it in for a different vehicle. Markio had given them $100,000 from his duffel bag, despite the fact that he hadn't asked them to shoot for him. He'd have whacked Binky himself if they hadn't jumped the gun.

Markio unfolded his MacBook Pro and opened the file he had his manuscript saved in. He waited for the plane to take to the skies and level off before he began to type, and he wasn't at all surprised when Nikkia lashed out at him not even five minutes later.

"You're not off the hook either," she said, leaning forward in her seat as her assistant/stewardess filled her crystal glass halfway up with cognac from a decanter. "Markio, I'm talking to you."

Markio looked up at her as Zia topped her drink off with a ball of ice and a splash of Pepsi. He'd brought his own beverage onto the private jet, a fresh cup of Wock and Sprite, and he sipped from it as he acknowledged Nikkia with a slight nod. The temperature inside the cabin was notably cool, though he could feel the heat from the vents slowly beginning to warm the air.

"You better get your priorities in order," Nikkia said, "You don't make plans with your woman and then try to cancel them so you can 'handle some'n in the streets.' You're supposed to be done living that lifestyle."

"I am," Markio lied. "I'm a bestselling author now. I write books, which is what I was doing when you so rudely interrupted me."

"Oh, please. All you do is sip Lean and smoke blunts and hang out with gang members. You've spent more money on weed than you've spent on investments. I'm not seeing any of the things you promised me the day you walked into my office last year."

"I told you what I was and who I was from the jump. When I walked into your office, I had a bullet lodged in the pile of hundreds I paid you with because I had been shot in the leg the night before. I was being investigated for three murders. That's why I hired you. Did you forget all that?"

Nikkia regarded him with a long, cold stare. Behind her, Mike and Leon's eyes widened at the breaking news that their stepfather had been investigated for three homicides in the past. Mike's favorite rapper was Lil Durk, and all Leon listened to was G Herbo; the closest they'd ever come to meeting a real life gunslinger was through their headphones.

The silent treatment continued for quite a while. Markio started typing again, stopped to peer thoughtfully out his window, typed out a few more paragraphs, then logged into Instagram to check his notifications.

His relationship with Nikkia had made him an overnight celebrity. Within minutes of them announcing that they were a couple, his IG following had grown from a little over three thousand people to more than twenty thousand, and that was six months ago. Now he was up to 3.7 million followers—nowhere near Nikkia's 42.3 million, but certainly much more than he'd ever anticipated. He'd been paid $50,000 just to make an appearance at a Detroit night club a couple of weeks ago. He had a few celebrity followers, including Nicole Beharie, the sexy brown-skinned actress from *American Violet*, and NBA great Kevin Durant. There were a lot of models and strippers in his DMs, hundreds of women who were just as beautiful as Nikkia, but he rarely even read their messages. He was nothing if he wasn't loyal, and Nikkia Staples had changed his life.

He uploaded a pic he had taken with the gang at one of Bankroll Reese's strip clubs two nights ago. It showed him sitting at a VIP table with a mountain of one-dollar bills in front of him. Ten thousand dollars' worth. He'd thrown every dollar at a freckle-faced redbone nicknamed Raven, and ridiculously thick caramel-complexioned girl named Malaysia. His sister, Shakia, had snapped the photo from the next table over, capturing both Raven and Malaysia as they bounced their big round asses in front of him. Markio's reason for posting the pic was beyond petty; he knew that Bam and Malaysia were dating, and he wanted to show just how easy it was to get to Bam's girl.

That reminded him. Raven had messaged him asking if he'd ever consider putting her on the cover of one of his books. She knew all the characters from his best-selling book series, and she'd been one of the many young Black women who had stood in line at his very first book signing back in September. She claimed that, aside from Ashley and Jaquavis's iconic *The Central* series, Markio's *The Bird Man* series were her favorite books.

He went to his inbox and replied to Raven's direct message: '*Yeah I might be able to put you on the covers for my next book series. Got $100k for you to make a move for me too. Hml #773-555-2212.*'

He plugged the charging cards into his two iPhones and looked up at Nikkia. The temperature inside the cabin was considerably warmer than it had been when they first boarded the jet half an hour ago. Zia was taking Nikkia's coat, hat, and scarf, revealing the skin-tight beige colored Ivy Park bodysuit she wore beneath it.

The outfit was breathtaking on Nikkia. A strategic slit across the stomach area exposed her flat abdomen. Her meaty thighs spread out wonderfully on the white leather seat beneath her, accentuating her tiny waistline. She had her own MacBook Pro on the table in front of her, typing on a legal brief, and she was already on her second drink. Her lips glistened with a beige gloss from Rihanna's Fenty Beauty line of cosmetics. Her hair was long and blonde and straight, done by Arrogant Tae, Atlanta's premier hairdresser, who she'd flown in on her private jet exclusively, for the hair appointment. Her fingernails were painted beige and pointed like claws. Her wristwatch was a diamond Patek worth $320,000, and she wore a diamond Infinity-link necklace around her neck. She was a boss bitch, the kind of woman high-end fashion designers paid to wear their brands, one of the most sought after criminal defense attorneys in the country, and she was all Markio's.

Markio licked his lips, pushing his laptop to the side and staring wantonly at Nikkia's luscious legs, while Zia sat across the aisle from them and told Kay and Buck about the day she got the chance to meet Quavo and Takeoff at an

Atlanta shopping mall a few weeks before Takeoff was shot and killed in Houston. She had her phone out, showing Buck the photos from her celebrity encounter. Leon was nodding to whatever music was playing in his headphones. Mike was watching an ESPN news update on Damar Hamlin's improving condition on the ceiling-mounted television. Markio was only vaguely aware of what everyone else was doing. He was high and he was inhaling the mouth-watering scent of Nikkia's Tom Ford Rose Prick perfume, fantasizing about tasting her wet pussy on the tip of his tongue. Her pussy always smelled like fresh fruit, like ripe peach that had just been picked from the tree and sliced in half, and she always gasped at the initial feel of his tongue on her clitoris.

Nikkia glanced at him as he was lifting his gaze from her legs to her face. Her hard expression had over the past twenty minutes softened into a cool, focused one. She curled her lips to the side, clearly reading his mind. She was like a psychic when it came to reading his thoughts.

"You know I love you, baby," he said, and bit down on his bottom lip.

"Nuh-uh. No, Markio. Don't even think about it. Get back to writing."

"I need to talk to you in private. I swear to God, it's important. Give me five minutes in the restroom."

Nikkia offered him a middle finger and he hastily returned to his typing, and over the next hour and forty minutes Markio worked on completing his manuscript and struggled to keep his mind of Nikkia's goodies. It was certainly a struggle. His dick hardened and softened, and hardened and softened and hardened again, until he could feel the wet slime of precum on the head of his lengthy magic stick.

The Gulfstream landed in Miami at 2:46 p.m. Four triple-white Chevy Suburbans drove onto the tarmac and parked beside the jet as its door was being opened. Descending the stairs behind Nikkia, Markio's eyes became fixed on a fifth vehicle—an odd-looking white Rolls Royce convertible that was pulling in behind the four suburbans.

"That's the most expensive car in the world," Nikkia said, sounding excited all of a sudden. "The Rolls Royce Boat Tail. Costs twenty-eight million."

The heat hit Markio like a sledgehammer as he continued down the stairs. Zia had folded his leather jacket away in one of Nikkia's suitcases, but he still had on the Dior sweats, not to mention the body armor he wore under his sweatshirt. He was carrying his two Louis Vuitton duffels, and as they were approaching the suburbans, six brawny young Hispanic men exited one of the SUVS and boarded the jet to remove the rest of their luggage.

And then it happened: an older Hispanic male chauffeur got out of the Rolls Royce Boat Tail and walked around it to open the passenger's side door, and the most famous woman on planet Earth emerged from the back seat, clad in tight-fitting white sequined minidress and towering six-inch heels, with fat round diamonds encircling her neck, wrists, and fingers. Her curves rivaled Kim Kardashian's—vastly sloping hips and ass and large perky breasts. Her fade was exceptionally gorgeous, more stunning than words could express, with the same high cheekbones and slant-eyes Asian features Nicki Minaj possessed, and the sexiest sapphire-green eyes Markio had ever seen.

It was Alexus Castilla, Queen A in the flesh, and she was walking right toward him.

**

The 1600 block of Trumbull Avenue was so crowded with mourners that Tammy had to park her eight-year-old Dodge Charger on the 1500 block and walk south, her boots crunching on the snow-packed sidewalks as she went. She kept her head down and her shoulders up against the biting cold, and all she could think about was the direct message she'd received from Markio Earl almost two hours ago:

'Got $10k for you to do some'n for me…'

The message kept replaying in her head as she walked across 16th Street, pulling her sturdy old red leather Pelle Pelle coat tight around her slender figure. Tammy was a cute young woman of twenty-four, an ex-scammer who'd called it quits after serving three years in federal prison for two counts of fraud and five counts of identity theft. Now all she did was pop pills, smoke weed, and drink hard liquor. She used her petite body to acquire the money and drugs that fed her habits, sometimes having sex with two or three men at once, if the money was right. She'd done other sinister things for money as well. Twice, she'd been the getaway driver in the armed robberies of local drug pharmacies. One time, her daughter's father, Vontrell "Ugly Lord" Maxwell, had paid her $1,200 to pull up on an opp of his and wait while he got out and shot the boy in the head. Another time, he'd paid her $2,000 to unlock the back door to the house of an older man she was dating who'd made a small fortune selling counterfeit designer handbags. Vontrell had crept in and robbed the man, pistol-whipping him until he gave up the loot.

But never had she been offered $10,000 to set someone up.

Markio hadn't said it would be a set-up, but Tammy knew the game. She'd seen Markio's sleek white Cullinan and his cousin Buck's white Range Rover whip up on Binky just before the gunfire began. It was no coincidence that he'd messaged her shortly afterwards, offering her ten thousand dollars to do something for him. That 'something' would be a set-up, of that she was certain. She was also certain that she would go along with whatever Markio wanted her to do. After all, he was Markio Earl, not just a notoriously ruthless gang member, but also a very rich one.

Tammy had been trying to get in good with Markio for months now. Vontrell wanted her to set him up, but that wasn't in her plans. She was going to make him fall in love if she ever got him alone in a room with her. She'd bite a hole in the condom before she slid it onto his dick and pray for a baby. Markio was the winning ticket she needed to get out of the ghetto. Markio and Bam were the two richest niggas in the hood, but Bam didn't have a girlfriend whose net worth exceeded two hundred million dollars. Plus, Bam had already fucked Tammy several times, in every hole she had, and four of his six sons had fucked her after that. He didn't want anything more to do with Tammy. Markio, on the other hand, had never seen her naked, and she had yet to fuck any of his family members, so she was in the clear with him. All she needed was an opportunity. She knew he liked girls with fat asses, and the Brazilian butt lift she'd get with $10,000 would give her the kind of body she needed to reel him in.

The crowd in the basement apartment of 1628 South Trumbull Avenue was huge. The building had belonged to Bam's grandmother until she died of a heart attack three weeks after Big Worm and Lil Worm's joint funeral, but she'd left behind a large family. Bam and Big Worm had a combined total of ten adult sons—though two of Worm's boys were dead now—and most of them had kids of their own. Bam also had two younger sisters, both of whom were currently pregnant. The majority of the people in the crowded basement apartment weren't even related to the Pattersons. They were just young gang members who'd grown up around Binky and his family. Two of Binky's baby-mamas were also present, as well as about twenty more girls in their late teens and early twenties. Binky's favorite drink had been Dusse, and there were bottles of it everywhere. Everyone seemed to have either a bottle or a clear plastic cup full of cognac, and Tammy quickly found herself a cup in the packed kitchen and filled it up to the rim.

Jock appeared next to her and wrapped an arm around her shoulders. "This shit crazy as hell," he said, speaking loudly to make himself heard over the cacophony of loud voices and even louder music. "I told Binky not to go fuckin' around with that nigga. Something I told Lil Worm. They didn't listen to me. That nigga, Markio, a gremlin. He'll whack a nigga in a heartbeat, and you know Buck and Kay on the same shit."

Tammy could think of nothing to say, so she just shook her head and drank from her cup.

"You know I was with Mannie and Lil Worm when they got smoked in Indiana," Jock went on. "They thought we could just run in Markio mama crib with no consequences. I had a bad feelin' about it, so I backed off the porch right when Lil Worm started to open the door. That's when the gunshots started. They shot Mannie and Lil Worm right through the door. Markio knew we was comin', and he had his people waitin' to blow us down. His nephew got off on self-defense. Two free bodies. And the whole time all that was goin' down, Markio was right here in this apartment, shootin' Big Worm in the face. That nigga's like John Wick. I don't know why Bam think that nigga—Esco—gon' be able to get the job done. That man gon' end up dead just like Big Worm, Lil Worm, Binky, Mannie, Ace, Lil Mark, and everybody else who done been dumb enough to cross Markio and his people.

Tammy looked up at Jock; his mention of Esco had gotten her attention. Esco was a high-ranking Conservative Vice Lord from the Low End. He'd recently moved into a house on the 16th and Lawndale, a block that the CVL's had controlled for decades. Esco and his gang were making good money down there, selling crack and meth and exotic marijuana.

"What do you mean 'Esco'?" Tammy asked, taking another swallow of cognac.

Jock looked around. There were more than a few sets of eyes on him. Everyone knew he'd been with Binky when the shooting went down, and they were starting to talk about it. Keeping his arm around Tammy's shoulders, he turned and walked her to the small hallway bathroom, and he didn't say another word until they were alone inside of it with the door closed and locked.

"Esco did some time in Indiana with Markio," he said, setting his cup down on the sink. "He say they had started callin' Markio "Chucky Lord" in the joint 'cause he was always stabbin' niggas up. I guess Esco think he can get close enough to whack the nigga. Bam got a quarter million on Markio's head and Esco said he'll take the hit. Claim he gon' get it done by the end of the week."

The news sent Tammy's eyebrows to the top of her forehead. She gulped down the rest of her drink in two long swallows, and waited for the wildfire it created in her throat to settle. Then she shook her head again and said, "I ain't gon' cap, I'll be made as hell if Markio got killed. That nigga from the hood, too. I mean, I know he was gone for a long-ass time, but it ain't like somebody ran him out the hood. He was in prison. He's a solid nigga, and he from right here on Trumbull, and he's a fucking author. Who else we got out here smart enough to write a whole goddamn book series?"

"I like the nigga, too," Jock admitted with a shrug of his bony shoulders. "But shit, it is what it is. He done got Bam mad. And I hate to say it, but two hundred and fifty thousand dollars might get the job done." He paused to light a Newport. "Then again, Markio got long money, too. He might put a bag on Bam head and get him knocked off first. It's the battle of the titans."

Tammy nodded and let out a long sigh. She had a nice buzz going. The liquor had warmed her up from the inside out, and suddenly she found herself recounting the talk she'd had with Jock earlier, right before Binky was gunned down. "When you gon' let me bite on that pussy?" was how he'd started the conversation, and that had immediately piqued her interest, because she'd just been telling Big Jessica that she hadn't had her pussy eaten in almost two months. The few guys who were offering were broke, and Tammy didn't do broke. She had a seven-year-old daughter at home, and she'd spent her last thousand dollars making sure her baby had a decent Christmas. If a nigga wasn't talking money, Tammy wasn't talking sex. She'd rather pleasure herself than to give a broke nigga some pussy, and if there was one thing she knew about Jock and the boys he ran with, it was that they were far from broke.

Jock was a tall boy, about 6'2" and no more than 135 pounds. Tammy was only 5'5" and she thought she might weigh more than he did. There was scarring on the right side of his dark brown face from a house fire he'd survived when he was a kid, and the black, circular scars of six old bullet wounds in his chest and stomach from a shooting he'd survived in the summer of 2021. He was just eighteen years old, but he'd lived a hard life, the sort of life that could break a man's spirit.

He dug in the right-hand pocket of his Amiri jeans and dragged out a thick, folded knot of cash; being close with the Pattersons certainly had its perks. Jock worked for Bam at a drug house on Spaulding Avenue, and Tammy knew that the boys who worked for Bam made anywhere from $500 to $1,000 a day. She knew this because last year she'd dated another one of Bam's workers for about six weeks, and she'd talked him into letting her hold his money. He'd come up with $500 every night, often complaining about the $1,000 a night the "overseers" received, and he ended up letting her keep $5,000 for herself when they broke up.

She'd been trying to sink her teeth into another one of Bam's workers ever since.

Jock thumbed through several hundreds and peeled three of them loose from the knot of cash, bringing a grateful smile to Tammy's pretty face as he handed her the three hundred.

"Here, this for you and Tonyjah. And for whatever we gon' eat tonight. I'm stayin' over your crib."

Tammy folded the bills and slipped them into the front left-hand pocket of her jeans. "I'll go and grab us some steaks," she said. "Just call me before you come over. Let me use the bathroom real quick."

Jock picked up his cup and left the bathroom, and Tammy locked the door before she went and sat down on the toilet lid, her hands trembling with excitement. It had nothing to do with Jock; he was a small fry in the grand scheme of things.

She took out her iPhone and *FaceTimed* Markio, and she gasped when he appeared on the screen just a few seconds later. He wore a handsome smile on his light brown face, a smile that was somehow both warm and cold. Tammy spied a private jet in the background, but what really excited her was all the ice Markio had around his neck.

"Crazy-ass nigga," she said, beaming.

"I take it you got my message," he said, and licked his lips.

Tammy wanted to ride those lips. She'd fantasized about it a hundred times already.

She nodded rapidly, like a bobblehead on meth. "I know the game. I know I'm only twenty-four but I'm far from new to this shit. And I got some info for you already. You know Jock, right?"

"Yeah. That's who I need you to set the pick on."

"No, no. Not him. He's not your problem. He actually likes you. It's Bam you need to be worried about—well, Bam and Esco. Jock just told me that Bam is supposed to be paying Esco two hundred and fifty thousand dollars to kill you. Esco said he could get it done by the end of the week."

"Yeah?" Markio's smile grew wider. And then he laughed, nodding as he did it. "Okay—Okay," he said, still laughing, while behind him a line of Hispanic men in white business suits carried several suitcases down the steps of the private jet.

It was during this laughter that Tammy realized something: she was attracted to Markio, but she was also deathly afraid of him. Her mind flashed back to the shooting that had killed Binky. She had been right on the other side of that Jeep. One of those bullets could have easily taken her life, and yet here Markio was, laughing like it was nothing.

"Boy, you are crazy," she said, really meaning it this time. "So when can I get my money? And how much do I get for all this? I mean, I did just tell you everything you needed to know."

"I'll have my lil sister bring it to you today. I got twenty thousand for you. And listen…" He paused, looking off to his left. Tammy could hear two women laughing and talking somewhere near him, and she wondered if one of them was that famous lawyer he was dating. When he finally turned back to the camera, he said, "I want you to pull up on Esco for me. Give that nigga some pussy or some'n. I'll give you another fifty thousand if you can set that pick. Just text this phone with the location, and don't tell nobody. I mean nobody. Not Big J, not your gay-ass baby daddy, not none of your—"

"Okay, okay. I get it, and I already know where he lives." Tammy leaped off the toilet lid, her face glowing with delight as she twirled a lock of hair around a fore finger. Someone knocked on the bathroom door, and she yelled for them to wait before lowering her voice to a near whisper. "He stay with Lenora on 16th and Lawndale, and he got a trap house on the same street, a bando toward the end of the block. Lil Devin and Po Boy work for him. I don't know if I can get too close to Esco. Lenora been hatin' on me ever since I fucked her baby daddy on Thanksgiving, but I know he got a crush on me 'cause he stay in my DMs, so I'll see."

Markio licked his lips again and smiled. "Well, get to work. I'll have my sister call you."

He ended the video call, and Tammy jumped up into the air, the way she'd done back in her high school days, when she was a cheerleader. She took a second to compose herself and then opened the door—and she found herself face to face with Shameka, Binky's fiancée and the mother of his infant son.

Shameka's red-eyed scowl wiped the smile right off Tammy's face.

"The hell got you so happy?" Shameka asked. Her eyes were bloodshot from crying, but she wasn't crying now. She was an unattractive dark-skinned girl with a body that had clearly been surgically enhanced. Binky's brother—Fat Boo—was standing right behind her, his huge beard hanging down over his Celine sweater.

"Just got a raise," Tammy said, averting her eyes. "Sorry. I know its' the wrong time to be smiling. I'm so sorry about Binky. Y'all know that was my nigga."

She slinked away, disappearing down the crowded hallway as she headed for the side door, and when she looked back she saw that Fat Boo was still watching her, his beady eyes asquint as he drank from a bottle of Dusse. Word on the street was that he had a meth house somewhere in Orland Park that made him tens of thousands every month, but Tammy had never tried to fuck with him. His reputation for beating on his women was known all throughout the city. He'd broken the jaw of his girlfriend—Jayla—for not turning off her phone at his father's funeral. Tammy hoped like hell he hadn't overheard her conversation with Markio.

Chapter 4

Markio and the boys—Kay, Buck, Mike, and Leon—loaded into the back of a single Suburban, while Nikkia joined Alexus in the Rolls Royce, and the motorcade of all-white vehicles left the airport in a hurry.

"Bullet Face used to have Alexus all through the hood," Buck said, cracking open a fresh pint of Wockhardt and pouring a fourth of it into his tall Styrofoam cup. "She really the one who put the family on. She had her people dump a truckload of bricks on Reecie Cup, and when he died, Bankroll Reese got everything."

Markio only nodded. He was preoccupied with his phone, googling the Rolls Royce Boat Tail. When it came up that the car really did cost $28 million, his jaw dropped a little. Dating Nikkia, he'd gotten pretty used to exorbitantly priced toys, but he'd never seen or even heard of a car worth that much money.

His mind switched back to the beef with Bam, and the situation with Esco. He couldn't speak on it in front of Leon and Mike, so he checked his Instagram inbox to see if Raven had seen his message. She hadn't. Markio considered the time of day and figured Raven had likely worked late into the night at Redbone's and had yet to awaken.

He thought of Esco, whose brother—Peanut—was a legend from the Low End area of the South Side of Chicago. Esco's father, a notorious drug lord and a former chief of the CVLs, was currently serving the equivalent of a life sentence in a federal prison, locked away with the likes of Jeff Fort and Larry Hoover in Florence, Colorado. Markio had first heard about Esco shortly after his arrival at Indiana State Prison, but he didn't meet Esco until he was sentenced to a year in the SHU, Indiana's super-max segregation unit. When Esco got out of prison a few months ago and reached out to Markio on social media, Markio had taken him out for a night on the town, and at the end of the night he'd blessed Esco with ten pounds of exotic bud and $20,000 in cash, purely off the strength of Esco's reputation as a stand-up Vice Lord.

Just then, as if his iPhone had synced with his thoughts, Markio got a Facebook Messenger notification saying he'd just received an inbox message from Esco. He tapped into the Messenger app and read it:

'Lord my girl and her people havin' a lil get together on 69th and Ashland this Tuesday night. They love yo books. I told her I know you and now her whole family wanna meet you. Can you slide through?'

A cold, nefarious grin spread slowly across Markio face. It was a smart move on Esco's part—get Markio way out south and ambush him there; that way, the heat would stay far away from the North Lawndale neighborhood. Everyone would assume the Black Disciples or some other South Side gang had done it, maybe out of retaliation for the BD he'd gone to prison for killing.

Mike and Leon, sitting on the second-row seats in front of Markio and his two cousins, had turned to look at Kay as he prepared his own cup of Wockhardt and cream soda. Kay was telling them about the Clermont Twins, two identical twin strippers from D.C. who'd spent two days with him at a hotel last week, and the boys were all ears, but as far as Markio was concerned, they could have been on another planet. He was focused solely on the message from Esco.

He put in his AirPods and vibed out to "Trap Like Me," a Bullet Face and Young Thug collaboration. Shutting his eyes, he imagined himself nudging Esco awake with the short barrel of his Draco, seeing the fear of God in Esco's eyes a millisecond before fire belched from the barrel and sent a barrage of 7.62x34 rounds through his head, knocking the corn-rowed braids from his head. How dare Esco betray the one outstanding gang member who'd blessed him when he came home from prison! Markio was the reason Esco was driving around the city in a blood-red Challenger, the reason he was stunting on Facebook in designer gear, the reason he was able to support his family.

Markio's thoughts wandered back to Bam, and he wondered what the rest of the Patterson family was up to. Were they also plotting against him? Were they preparing to attack someone in his family? The majority of Markio's family had moved out of the hood, but there were some stragglers. His older brother—Boadie—the black sheep of his father's children, was addicted to smoking embalming fluid and was often found stumbling around the neighborhood, wacked out of his mind. Lil Bill, another one of Markio's half brothers, lived with his girlfriend Poochie on 16th and St. Louis, just across the alleyway from the Patterson family's Trumbull Avenue building, but Lil Bill and Poochie were in Los Angeles, blowing through the $100,000 Markio had gifted Lil Bill for Christmas. Buck and his girlfriend—Lana—along with their ten-year-old daughter whose nickname was Marcie, lived on 15th and Homan. Kay owned a house three blocks down from them, off 15th and Drake. Bam and his people could easily slide on one of them.

Markio nodded and increased the volume on the music he was listening to. Feeling relatively at ease about his family's safety, he shut his eyes again and this time his world went black. He dozed for a long while; the Wockhardt had that effect on him.

When he came to, the Suburban was trailing the Rolls-Royce Boat Tail into the driveway of the most extravagant home he'd ever seen, and considering the fact that he'd been living with Nikkia at her lavish Burr Ridge castle for the past couple of months, that was saying something.

They were escorted inside by the queen herself, and Markio noted that Alexus Castilla resembled Alexis Skyy from the back. Her ass was big and round and incredibly soft-looking. She and Nikkia were lost in conversation, discussing the Miami Beach housing market, and how Bullet Face had bet $200 million on the Bills versus Patriots game to celebrate Damar Hamlin's recovery.

It took Markio a moment to realize that they were walking through the world-renowned Versace Mansion. He remembered reading in a DuPont Registry magazine that Alexus had purchased the famous home, though he couldn't recall the price she'd allegedly paid for it. He thought it might've been $75 million. Looking around at the embroidered Versace curtains hanging down over all the tall windows, and the silky Versace Fabric on the sofas and chairs and rugs, and the Versace emblems on the rich Italian marble floors they were walking across, he thought it might be worth every penny.

"Man, cousin," Kay said, his high-yellow face aglow with amazement, "this shit right here is unbelievable. I ain't never seen nothin' like this in my life. This a whole nother level of money right here."

"On Bay-Bay grave," Buck agreed, his eyes flicking left and right, high and low.

They were led up a spiral staircase and down a wide hallway and around a bend, and Alexus stopped in the middle of a hallway with enormous bedrooms on both sides. As the white-suited men rolled their suitcases into the bedrooms, Alexus turned to Markio and gave him an appraising glance. She had smiled and waved at him when Nikkia introduced him as her boyfriend at the airport, but this look was different.

"You and I need to have a talk," she said. "Follow me. The rest of y'all can go ahead and get settled in."

Markio's eyebrows shot skyward, and Nikkia said, "Oh, Lord Jesus. Protect my man."

"Protect me?" Markio said, knitting his brow and handing one of his duffels to Buck.

Alexus was already walking off, flanked by four Hispanic men in impeccable white three-piece suits, and since no one offered an explanation for Nikkia's impromptu prayer, Markio went and caught up with Alexus as she headed back in the direction from which they'd come. He was carrying the heavier of his two large duffel bags, the one that held his Draco, his two .40 caliber Glocks, and $300,000 in cash.

"So," Alexus asked, looking over at him, "what do you have in mind for my friend? You plan on proposing anytime soon? I mean, yesterday made six months. What are you waiting for?"

Markio chuckled once. "What?" He chuckled again. Licked his lips. Tried to calm his nerves. His heart was booming in his chest. There was only one Black woman in the world who was as powerful and influential as Alexus Castilla, and that was Beyonce. "First off," Markio said, finding his voice, "it's nice to meet you. I used to have a picture of you taped to my wall when I was in prison, but I never thought I'd actually get to meet you. Niggas wouldn't even believe me if I told 'em where I'm at right now. Is Bullet Face here, too?"

"I ask the questions." Alexus spoke in a surprisingly authoritative tone of voice. She stopped at the head of the staircase and turned to face Markio, folding her arms over her buxom chest. The big round white diamonds in her necklace were likely worth millions; they shimmered brilliantly in the sunlight spilling down from the skylight. The four Hispanic men continued on down the stairs, but they halted after descending the first couple of steps. Markio thought they moved with the swift fluidity of trained soldiers.

"My bad," Markio said, grinning from ear to ear as he turned to Face Alexus. "I got choo. You ask the questions. Ask away."

"Hm!" Alexus drew her lips thin and looked him up and down. She towered over him in her tall, white leather heels. "Blake was short like you when I first met him. Then the bastard had a growth spurt and started cheating like crazy. I had to kidnap his side bitch and threaten to cut her open with a chainsaw to get him in line. Had a few of the other ones killed. He's been on the right track ever since."

Yeah, right, Markio thought. He'd heard rumors that Alexus was an elite member of Mexico's Matamoros Drug Cartel, but he didn't believe any of it. No one did. It was just like the rumor that Alexus was the head of the Illuminati, and the rumor the Matamoros Cartel was originally called the Castilla Cartel; or the insane theory that Quavo had sacrificed Takeoff in the name of Satanism. None of it was even slightly believable. Markio lived in reality. Anyone who thought a person as wealthy as Alexus was involved in criminal activity may as well believe Tupac was still alive.

"I don't want no smoke, Queen A," he said, smiling. "But for the record, though, I love Nikkia. Loved her ever since I was a kid. And yes, I do plan on proposing. Just ain't did it yet."

"Well, don't keep her waiting. You're lucky she even gave you a chance." Alexus glanced at her diamond wristwatch. It was a Richard Mille, just like the one Nikkia wore. "So, how many pounds of that weed do you have left? Why haven't you re-upped?"

Markio's head jerked back. "What weed? I don't sell drugs," he said haltingly.

"Sure, you don't, but your boy Reggie went from copping a hundred pounds at a time to copping two thousand pounds. You didn't think we'd look into that? She who he had that load delivered to? You've got him and your nephew Tyquan Holton shipping the pounds to buyers through the mail. You've kept the load at that big house you're renting in Valparaiso, and Tyquan stays there with his girlfriend. But you don't trust him with it so you keep the basement door locked, and you and Reggie are the only ones with the keys to unlock it."

Markio's jaw became unhinged. He looked at Alexus with his mouth wide open, his eyes replete with disbelief. How in the fuck did she know so much about his operation? He hadn't even told Nikkia about the pounds of exotic bud he'd been selling; she was under the impression that he was still living off the $5 million he'd found in Big Worm's storage locker.

Or at least he hoped she was under that impression.

"Don't worry," Alexus said, a sneaky smile playing at the corners of her mouth. "I didn't tell her. She'd go nuts if she knew. Especially if she knew I was involved." She began to walk down the stairs, moving slowly, a step and a pause. "You know, you'd be surprised how many people will actually pay you if you just front them the product. You're waiting on those up-front payments, and it's slowing down your business."

"How you know what I'm doing?" Markio asked defensively, because Alexus was right on every assumption.

"We'll talk about that later," she said, waving off the question with a flutter of her flawlessly manicured fingers. "First thing first. Is there anything else you need? Are you ready for another load of Black Cherry Gelato? We do have other strains, but Black Cherry Gelato is the most popular one we have right now. If you want bricks of coke, I'll need twenty thousand dollars per kilo, and you'll need to buy at least a hundred of them. Kilos of heroin and fentanyl go for fifty grand each—same deal, you'll need to buy at least a hundred bricks, and I'll front you whatever you buy. You can step on every kilo you get because none of them will be cut when you receive them, and I do mean none of them. That's my personal guarantee. Pure cocaine, pure heroin, pure fentanyl. What do you say? You in or you out?"

Markio didn't know what to say. Either this was an elaborate set-up by some federal agency or Alexus really was the notorious drug-trafficker she was rumored to be. The former possibility seemed illogical; if the Feds knew where his stash house was located, what he had stashed in it, and who he had mailing it out to his clientele, it almost certainly would have been raided by now. Plus, there was no way that Alexus, the wife of America's most famous gangsta rapper, was working with the Feds.

Which left the latter possibility: Alexus Castilla was indeed a member of the infamously ruthless Matamoros Cartel, and with a reported net worth of almost three hundred billion dollars, she was likely the drug cartel's leading lady, if not the top boss.

Markio thought back to all the news stories he'd seen and read about Alexus and her family when he was in prison. He remembered reading in *Time* magazine that her father, Juan "Papi" Castilla, was once indicted for allegedly running the Matamoros Cartel. And of course there was Papi's sister Jenny, the deadly terrorist who'd murdered dozens of innocent Americans before setting off a massive explosion in Washington D.C. that had practically leveled the city, killing thousands more. There were some unexplained FBI raids on Alexus and Blake's homes, and Blake "Bullet Face" King was once arrested for a long list of homicides, though Britney Bostic—Nikkia's partner at the Bostic and Staples law firm—had gotten those charges dismissed. There was also the time when Alexus opened fire on Blake's tour bus during a live taping of TMZ. The footage had instantly gone viral, and all the inmates in prison with Markio had gone wild, saying how they'd known all along that Alexus was a real gangsta bitch. That was the day Markio had taped a magazine photo of Alexus to the wall in his prison cell.

But he'd never known just how deeply Alexus was tied into the streets until now.

"I'll uhh…I'll think on it and get back to you," he said, still too stunned by the revelation to even consider making decisions.

But the wheels were already turning in his head. Pure cocaine—he knew several men he could sell bricks of that to, starting with Small Body, a diamond-mouthed dope boy from Indianapolis's 40th and Boulevard neighborhood. Superstar street niggas like Yo Gotti, EST Gee, and Zack "Z-Bo" Randolph hung out in Small Body's hood whenever they were in town, because it was an area where real trap niggas were known to make millions. Markio knew he'd be able to dump the whole load of cocaine bricks on Small Body. And as for the heroin, he'd easily be able to get those off for $80,000 a ki, and that was after he stretched each kilo into three or four kilos. The Fentanyl—he could stretch even further.

"Shit," he muttered, beaming as they continued down the staircase. "You got me thinkin' now."

"Trappin' ain't dead, y'all niggas just scared," Alexus sang, quoting Jeezy, smiling harder than Markio, stopping to wind her hips in a sexy little dance in the middle of the staircase. "Whatever you decide, just text me saying you'd like to have a business lunch. Don't even come close to mentioning drugs."

"Come on, now I know better than that."

"I know you do. The FBI has been tailing you for the past six months, and they haven't uncovered a thing."

"Huh?" Markio looked at her. They were approaching the foot of the staircase. "How you know that?"

"I know a lot of things. We've got multiple sources inside the FBI, the DEA, the ATF, even the DOJ. I know when they're onto us before they do. You're being investigated for several murders in Michigan City and two more murders in Chicago, all of which took place on July sixth and July seventh of last year. I had your name put through the federal database the night you and Nikkia started dating, just in case they were trying to set my girl up with a rat. I actually found out your full name before she even told me about you. Some girl named Shamara Mosley had posted your name under a video of you and Nikkia on The Shade Room's Instagram page."

"So Nikkia knows all about you, huh?" Markio asked. They were on the main floor now, strolling side by side across the marble. The distinct scent of exotic marijuana was heavy in the air.

Alexus nodded. "Of course she knows. She's been around from the very beginning. Not that she'd ever rat me out. We're like sisters. Plus…well, she knows what would happen."

Alexus shrugged and reached out to one of the burly Hispanic men walking next to her. They were bodyguards, Markio decided. One of them handed Alexus an iPhone. She stopped again ten feet from a door marked "Studio A." She accessed the iPhone's camera and handed it back to the bodyguard. She posed. Markio smiled. The bodyguard snapped a couple of photos and then handed the phone back to Alexus. She then began to type, speaking out loud as she did it.

"Look…who…came to visit me…today. Exclamation mark. Book emoji. Fire emoji."

Markio's mouth fell open again. Alexus was by far the most influential woman on Instagram, with well over four hundred million followers, though she only followed five accounts herself: Bullet Face, Beyonce, Michelle Obama, MTN (short for the Minority Television Network, which Alexus owned, and Rita Mae Bishop, the Emmy-winning daytime talk show host who also happened to be Alexus's mother.

"I'm about to get you another few million followers," Alexus stated proudly as she uploaded the photo.

"There will be a lot of offers on the table for you from this one post. Take advantage of them."

"Thanks. I appreciate it," Markio said, knowing there was truth in her words. A photo of himself beside Alexus, posted to Alexus' IG page, would bring unprecedented attention to his books.

"Show me how much you appreciate it by accepting my offer." Alexus handed her iPhone back to the bodyguard and stood in front of Markio with her hands planted on her hips. "Get yourself some real money. If you're gonna be in the streets, make that shit count. Don't get seven figures and become content. Stay hungry. I'm up to twelve figures and I'm still hungry."

"So what do you suggest I do?"

"You're already doing it, Markio. You've got a low-key stash house in a secret location. There's even an old farmhouse on the property that's perfect for storing large loads, and it's way out on a rural back road, where no one will go. We could send you loads every week."

"I'll take you up on that offer," Markio said, after some thought. "A hundred bricks of that girl and another thousand pounds of zah. And I'll give you the three million up front."

Alexus shook her head in disagreement. "Two hundred kilos, and two thousand pounds of BCG. You'll owe me the other three million on the back end."

Markio took out one of his own iPhones and accessed the calculator to crunch the numbers. Alexus watched him do it. The stench of high-grade marijuana grew stronger by the second, making Markio fiend for a puff as he punched in the cocaine numbers and multiplied, then punched in the exotic weed numbers and multiplied, then subtracted his investment. The final number made him cringe.

"On second thought," he said, lowering the phone to his side, "I'll just stick with the zah. It's too much risk fuckin' with the soft and not enough reward. Even if I sold the bricks for thirty-five thousand apiece, that wouldn't be about seven million. I'd have to cut the dope just to double my money."

"Or you could just be content with the three million you'd pocket, and your clientele would surely be appreciative of the pure fishscale they'll be getting," Alexus reasoned.

"You're right. But if I just buy the two thousand bows, and sell each bow for thirty-five hundred, that would be seven million off a two million-dollar investment. That profit margin makes a lot more sense to me. Less risky, too. Feds ain't lookin' for no weed-dealers."

"Okay." Alexus began to pace from one side of the wide hallway to the other, holding the second knuckle of her forefinger between her teeth, thinking. "Okay," she said a short time later. "What if I gave you the first two hundred kilos for twelve instead of twenty, and after that I went up to the sixteen and stay there? That sound better?"

"Hell yeah." Markio's handsome grin made an abrupt return, and he nodded ecstatically. "I'm all the way with that."

Alexus pumped her fist triumphantly, then took his phone and saved a number in his contacts list under the name *Queen*.

"I use a prepaid phone for this sort of thing. I switch the number once a week and switch phones about once a month. I'll keep you updated on the new numbers."

"I do the same thing all the time."

"Smart man." She gave his trap phone back. "You should use two separate phones, though. Keep one consistent number for legitimate business calls and the other one—"

"I do that, too." Markio was about to pocket the phone, but it vibrated in his hand. He read the notification and saw that it was a new text message: 'This Raven, just waking up. Call me when you get a chance."

"Okay," Alexus said. "You might want to give your nephew a call. That shipment'll be there in about an hour or so. Make sure he's home to receive it."

"Wait," Markio said, squinting. "How you know I was gon' accept the offer?"

"I've done my research on you," she explained. "You're a born and bred hustler. It's in your DNA. My husband still talks with a lot of his family in Indiana. He knows people who were in prison with you, people who knew you in Michigan City before you moved back to Chicago. I knew you'd take the offer. Only thing I didn't foresee was you turning down the heroin and Fentanyl—I've got fifty bricks of each in that load with your coke and weed, but you can just send them back. I'll send someone to pick them up."

"Nah, I'll keep 'em." Markio smiled appreciatively. "You did me a favor. I'll do you a favor."

"*Plato o plomo*," Alexus replied, and Markio had no clue what the hell it meant but he assumed it was something good, so he nodded in agreement, and they shook hands. "If Nikkia asks, she added, "I only asked about your intentions with her. And don't tell anyone else about this little talk of ours. Not even your two cousins up there, even though I remember them from back when I used to do business with Reesie Cup. Discretion is everything."

Markio gave another nod and was starting to turn back toward the staircase when the door marked "Studio A" swung open and a second famous face swaggered out into the hallway. It was Blake "Bullet Face" King. Beyond him, inside the smoke-clouded studio, Markio caught a quick glimpse of Atlanta rap superstar: Future, and Chicago drill rap star—G-Herbo. They were seated in leather swivel chairs behind the soundboard while a phalanx of young street niggas stood around them, rolling blunts, sipping Lean from Styrofoam cups, and vibing to the music. The two rap legends looked Markio's way, and then Bullet Face pulled the door shut.

"The man of the hour," he said, crossing the hall to shake Markio's hand. He had a gritty, aggressive baritone, and he caught Markio by surprise when he performed the TVL handshake flawlessly. "You know I'm from C. They say you been slumpin' shit out there. Say you like I used to be on them hoe-ass niggas, standin' on they necks."

Markio chuckled twice. "Yeah, some'n like that. I'm just tryna get some money. Niggas be in the way out there. Actin' like I'm goin' for that bullshit. I ain't never went, on Vice Lord."

Blake gave a subtle nod. He had a peculiar, sort of half-grin that showcased a few of the diamond teeth on one side of his mouth. He'd grown his hair into thick dreadlocks that hung down past the shoulders of his white Prada T-shirt. The pockets of his off-white sweat shorts bulged with cash bundles; Markio knew this because his sweatpants pockets held bulges of the same shape and width. Like Alexus, Blake wore fat round diamonds around his neck and wrists that made Markio's Cuban-links look like costume jewelry. Like Markio, Blake toted a Glock with a 30-shot extended clip, only Markio's was in his heavy duffel bag, and Blake's was on his hip.

"You know what's crazy?" Blake asked, as Alexus stood off to the side, hands on her slim waist, her sexy green eyes darting from Markio to her husband. "I'm from Michigan City, but I moved to Chicago and fucked with the Travelers in yo' hood—at the start of my career, I mean. And you from Chicago, but moved to MC and fucked with them niggas in my hood."

"Yeah, I met your brother before I went to the joint. Cool nigga. I used to trap in your hood. Me. Tooter, Snotts, Blubb, Straw, Rice G. Young D. We was all out there trappin'."

"All my Dub Life niggas," Blake said proudly. For a fleeting moment, his half-grin grew into a full-on smile. Then it faded away, and he added, "That was years ago. I had to fall back from them niggas to stay out the Feds. I was movin' bricks, and them niggas, was too hot, catchin' cases left and right. Plus, I was at war with them 10th street niggas. Then I moved to Chicago and fell out with Sosa n'em. I had to fall back and focus on the music. Now all I do is fuck with my artists and a few other real niggas in th industry. I heard you used to rap. You need to jump in the booth with me."

"Nah." Markio shook his head. "I'm a shooter, bruh. A trapper and a shooter, that's it. If not for all the time I did in the joint, I wouldn't have even started writin' them books. I did that shit for all the real niggas who ain't never comin' home, and for all my dead homies. For Cup and Lil Cholly. For my cousin—Have—and my uncle, Lil Joe."

Blake's million-dollar smile returned. "Cup was my nigga! That's how I became a Vice Lord, fuckin with him. We had our issues here and there, but we made millions in the streets together. That's why his son—Bankroll Reese— got all that money. He got that bread from all the bricks we flooded his daddy with."

"Bankroll Reese my lil cousin," Markio said.

"Yeah, wifey told me." Blake glanced at his diamond wristwatch; Markio had no idea what kind of watch it was but it looked like it might cost a few million dollars. "I gotta get back in here and finish this mix tape. It's open for you, if you ever wanna go in. I'll sign you to MBM. I don't care how hard you is in the booth; I know you'll whack some'n, and that's all that matters to me. I fuck with all the killers."

"I'll think about it," Markio said, feeling his phone vibrate in his pocket as he shook up with the billionaire drill rapper a second time and then watched him disappear back into the studio.

The record deal was a tempting offer—years ago, Markio had loved writing music, but he was knee-deep in the streets now. It was hard enough being with a famous lawyer like Nikkia. Within the first few months of them dating, he'd been hounded by paparazzi several time. The photos later ended up on numerous blog sites, as well as a number of gossip magazines. It was a good thing he wore sunglasses; otherwise, they'd have seen how bloodshot his eyes were from all the blunts he smoked. He was selling hundreds of pounds of exotic weed right under their noses, apparently while the Feds were watching his every move. Becoming a rapper, signing to one of the hottest record labels in the industry, would lead to even more unwanted attention.

Markio also felt he was too old to be starting a rap career. He was three weeks away from his thirty-sixth birthday. And besides, he was already living the life of a rap star, making millions of dollars, driving a $500,000 Rolls Royce Cullinan, dripping in ice and designer gear. He was feeding his entire family. His novels were best-sellers. There was no sense in doing anything to bring more heat to his operation.

He looked at Alexus and smirked. She was watching him, her arms folded over her breasts now. She smelled so good and she was so fucking beautiful. He decided to get away from her before she caught him looking at her in a suggestive way, and as he turned and walked back toward the staircase, pulling out his phone, he saw that her gaze hadn't wavered. She stared after him until they lost sight of each other.

"Goddamn, that bitch bad," Markio muttered out loud, finally looking at his phone screen. He had missed a video call from his ex-girlfriend—Whitney. She didn't have his phone number, so she'd called him through Instagram, where her following had also grown. She was up to 1.7 million followers, thanks to her burgeoning line of cosmetics and her friendship with Bunny XXX, a famous porn star from Chicago who'd gained fame after one of her insane blowjob videos went viral a few years back. The internet had nicknamed Bunny XXX the Throat Goat, and despite the fact that she was now his ex's bestie, Markio found himself watching Bunny's videos quite often.

He paused at the top of the staircase and returned the video call, putting on a blank expression when she answered. Whitney was a badass yellowbone—she was no Alexus, but she was damn close. He'd broken it off after she had some young niggas break in his house in an attempt to steal his money. They hadn't succeeded, but the act itself had irreparably damaged his relationship with Whitney and her four children. He hadn't spoken on the phone with either of them ever since, though he sometimes lurked on Whitney's page. She was living her best life down here in Miami, staying in an enormous mansion that belonged to Bunny's NFL star boyfriend—Keondre Muck.

He could see that Whitney was walking around inside of her new cosmetics store; in the background, orange tubes of lip gloss lined the shelves, and the orange-on-white *iKiss Kosmetics* logo was everywhere.

"I see you doing good down here," Markio said, doing his best to remain unreadable.

"What do you mean 'down here'? You in Miami already?"

Markio nodded. "Landed a lil' while ago. We're at the Versace Mansion with Alexus and Bullet Face."

"Yeah the fuck right. And I'm here with Barack and Michelle.

"On Vice Lord I'm not lyin'." He focused on the background. "I like what you did with the iKiss store. Been seeing the videos and pictures on IG. I'm proud of you, for real for real. On the gang, I was watching a video on You Tube the other day and a commercial for iKiss popped up. Couldn't believe it. I had to show my nigga—Perk."

"Yeah, we've put a lot of money into advertising. Bunny talked Keondre into paying five million to lock in a Super bowl ad for me. I have to pay it back, but that'll be nothing. We're already up to over seven hundred thousand dollars in month online sales. I'm thinking of doing an IPO sometime next year or maybe even later this year, which will make me a very rich bitch. We just moved our production into a twenty-thousand-square foot factory in Jacksonville. I changed the spelling of cosmetics, switched the C to a K, and we made a few other minor changes to increase sales. It's all working out better than I ever expected."

"I'm proud of you, Whitney. I really am. I'll be there at the grand opening."

"I hope you're bringing my two and a half million dollars with you. I really do need it. I have leases to pay on all these buildings, and you wouldn't believe me if I told you how much it costs to advertise in Vogue magazine. I need—"

Whitney shut up and sucked her teeth crossly when Markio began to laugh.

"Are you serious right now?" he asked.

"Yes, I'm fuckin' serious," she snapped, "You only gave me fifty thousand dollars, one percent of five million you got out of that locker. I had to kill someone for trying to kidnap me about that money. And we were together."

"I paid for that locker, Whitney. All you did was sign for it. I paid for it because I needed the furniture. And I would've given you way more than that fifty thousand if you hadn't had Flocka and Millie Mel break in my house to try to steal the money."

"Whatever. You never would've known about that storage auction if I hadn't told you about it. I want my cut, Markio. This is my last time asking."

"Good. That mean it'll be my last time sayin' no. Fuck you thought I was gon' say? '*I'm sorry, baby. I got that two and a half million for you.*' Get the fuck outta here. You can't game me, nigga. You owe me two million for all the free game I gave yo' ungrateful ass. Don't call me no mo'. I was tryna be nice and support yo' stupid ass, but fuck you and that grand openin'. You an iKiss-this-dick, bitch."

"Remember that," she said threateningly, and ended the video call.

Markio started off toward the bedrooms, texting on his trap phone and putting all thoughts of Whitney Clarrett out of his mind.

He'd underestimated her before, and though he didn't know it, he'd just done it again.

Chapter 5

There were far too many CPD vehicles traversing the ice-cold streets of North Lawndale in the wake of Binky's murder. Bam had to shut down shop at three of his trap houses for the day, and now in an Escalade ESV, with his sons—Spin and Jinx—in the SUV with him, he made a decision.

"We ain't gon' slide until sundown," he said as Malaysia turned southbound onto Kedzie Avenue. "It's way too hot out here right now. I done seen six police cars in ten minutes."

And as he said it, a CPD Tahoe turned off of Douglas Boulevard and rumbled past them. Malaysia slowed down a bit. She was dressed in dark colors like her three passengers, only she didn't wear a ski-mask on the top of her head like they did.

"Fat Boo say he about to set Lil Bill and Poochie's building on fire," said 23 year-old Desmond "Spin" Patterson from behind Bam. He was tall and dark like his father. He suffered from alopecia, which left him with absolutely no hair his body, so he'd gotten a set of eyebrows inked onto his face. He'd earned his nickname seven summers ago, when his "Baby T Blood Gang" set of TVLs were at war with the "Rich Way" CVLs. He'd driven down Ridgeway and opened fire on his opps with a 30-shot .45 caliber Ruger, then circled the block twice more, until he finally shot and killed Gang Baby, one of the deadliest opps his gang had ever faced.

"Tell him to do it," Bam said through clenched teeth. "Tell him I said burn that bitch down. And if that white Benz Markio gave Lil Bill parked out there, burn that up, too. Fuck them niggas."

Bam's right hand was clenched tight around a stolen Glock 19 with a 50-round drum and green laser sighting. Although the Glocks his sons toted in the back seat were different models, theirs had drums and switches just like Bam's, which meant the three of them had a hundred and fifty rounds of fully-automatic gunfire for Markio when they caught him.

Bam was undecided on the rest of Markio's family. The Earls and Pattersons were closely tied, but this was war. If either of Markio's cousins got involved, Bam would put price tags on their heads as well. He was reluctant to get Kay and Buck whacked; they were not only two of his best friends but also two of his most loyal gang members, real street niggas he'd gone through a lot with over the years. But there was no forgiving Markio. Bam had already offered $250,000 to two other Vice Lords to kill Markio, and he couldn't wait to get the call from one of them saying the job was done.

***

Ceno and Lud Foe were both 4 Corner Hustlers, and they were two of the three most successful rap artists from their west side neighborhood. Ceno and his brother—Trav— (a TVL) comprised the rap group *Sicka Mob*. Lud Foe was a solo rap artist, though he'd recently released a collaborative mixtape with an Englewood GD to address their respective beefs with the O-Block BDs.

Today, though, they were posted up at Buck's house on 15th and Homan to address another beef: the TVLs on 16th and Trumbull were talking about retaliating against the TVLs and 4 CHs on 154 and Homan over Binky's murder. It was an odd situation, because they were all essentially members of the same gang, though they ran in different circles. They had all gone to war with other local street gangs in the past, but never had they gone at each other. Nobody knew what to do, but the one thing all the gang members at Buck's house agreed on was that there would be gunshots if anybody tried to harm Buck or his younger brother Kay—or even Markio, who'd gone to prison for a murder when most of them were just kids.

Lud Foe and Sicko Mobb always flipped the money they made from doing shows by investing it into the tax-free drug game. Here, lately, they'd been buying pounds of Black Cherry Gelato from Markio and selling them for a profit. No one ever hesitated to drop $6,000 for a pound of the sticky exotic bud, and it was easy to break down a pound and charge twenty dollars per gram, making almost nine thousand dollars off the pound. Markio only charged them $4,500 per pound, which left them with a lot of room for profit. Ceno had already bought and sold thirty pounds, and Lud Foe had gone through twice that number since mid-November. They were both up six figures because of Markio. There was no way in hell they were going to just sit by and let him get smoked.

There were seventeen gang members gathered inside Buck's home, and just as many guns. Buck's girlfriend, Lana, had taken their daughter to his mother's house and returned with several of her female friends and numerous bottles of hard liquor, but hardly any of the boys were drinking, though there were plenty of blunts in rotation.

"On Fo'nem grave," Lud Foe said, screwing a sound suppressor into the barrel of his Mac-11 machine pistol, as he sat in a ladder-back chair he'd carried into the living room from the kitchen, "if one o'dem niggas ride through this bitch, I'm lettin' off this whole fifty clip."

"I ain't never like that nigga Binky anyway," Ceno muttered. He was standing at the living room window, looking out through the blinds, his eyes swinging from side to side as he watched every passing vehicle. "He always played that tough role 'cause his daddy had all that money. I told him that spoiled shit was gon' catch up to him one day. He ain't believe me."

Lil James, a 37-year-old with the same dark brown complexion as Ceno, stood up from the sofa, tucking his 30-shot Smith and Wesson pistol in the front of his designer jeans. "Fuck all this sittin' around. I'm in traffic. I'ma slide over there and see what they on."

The ember of the end of Ceno's blunt glowed red as he filled his mouth with smoke. He nodded in agreement with Lil James. There were a lot of police cars patrolling the neighborhood, but there was no sense in prolonging the inevitable. Besides, there was no way the police could catch them in the cars they owned.

"Fuck it, let's slide," Ceno said, passing the blunt to his brother—Trav. "What's the worst that could happen?"

***

"Boadie! Boadie! Bitch ass nigga, I know you hear me, Boadie!"

Boadie was standing on the sidewalk near the corner of 16th and Homan Avenue, bent over at the waist, his legs wobbling uncontrollably. The cold was biting, but he hardly felt it, and the thermal underwear he wore under his Palm Angels jogger had little to do with his warmth. Prior to leaving his girlfriend Tasha's house, he'd dipped a cigarette in a bottle of embalming fluid, and he'd smoked it with her as they sat in her SUV, a brand new GMC Acadia he'd bought for her with the $50,000 his younger brother, Markio, had gifted him for Christmas. Tasha was supposed to have driven him to his cousin Buck's house, but he couldn't remember anything after that. Looking down at the salt and melted snow between his Jordan sneakers, it registered in his drug-clouded brain that he was outside, on a sidewalk somewhere, though he had no clue how he'd gotten there.

Someone was calling his name, screaming his name, but he couldn't lift his head to see who it was. Some part of his subconscious had ordered his cold black hands into his pants pocket, and now they were stuck there. His head jerked about sporadically, just like his legs. He tried vehemently to raise his head, concentrating with all his available brain power, all to no avail.

And then someone helped him do it. A large, powerful hand clamped down on the nape of Boadie's neck and yanked him upright. His dilated pupils scanned the street in front of him, and he was glad to see that he had at least made it to Buck's block. Buck's house was across the street and four houses down, the front door just swinging open. He could only see this in his periphery, his body still going through a period of shaky spasms, as if he'd suddenly come down with a debilitating case of Parkinson's disease. Plus, there was something hard being pressed against the right side of his face, preventing him from turning to look north up Homan Avenue even if he could.

A cold, ominous voice in his right ear said, "Where the fuck Markio at?"

It was a familiar voice, but Boadie was far too high to figure out who it belonged to. Even though he could clearly see Shameka—a big bootied girl whose throat he'd fucked a couple of times since he'd moved from his south side neighborhood to be closer to his father's family—waiting at the curb inside Fat Boo's mustard-yellow BMW X6, his mind was too fuggy to make a connection.

"I'ma ask you one more time," the malevolent voice said, and this time Boadie smelled the pungent stench of alcohol on the speaker's breath. "Where the fuck is that bitch-ass nigga Markio? Where he live at? Either you tell me that or I'ma kill yo' ass right on this sidewalk."

Boadie's eyes went wide with fear as the threat suddenly registered in his drug-muddled brain. The fear was galvanizing enough to cause his hands to pull free of his pockets, and he swung his arm in the direction of the invisible threat. Only the threat wasn't invisible, because the back of his hand made hard contact with something thick and bushy, and as he fell away he managed to look and see that he had backhanded a man with a heavy beard.

The man was Fat Boo, Bam's nephew, Boadie realized. Which is when another piece of the puzzle fell into place: Boadie's brother, Markio, had done something to Binky, and Buck had texted Boadie a warning to be careful around Binky's family. It was the whole reason Boadie had wanted Tasha to bring him to Buck's house in the first place. He'd wanted to get the details of what had happened.

Boadie tried without much success to get his body under control as he landed on his ass. Fat Boo had also gone down, and he was raising a chrome-plated handgun as he struggled to find his footing, leveling the barrel on Boadie's face. Boadie's right hand came up to shield his face as Fat Boo bit down on his bottom lip and pulled the trigger. The gun flashed and boomed. Boadie felt a sudden sting in his forearm, and his head jerked sideways as a bullet tore through his lower jaw. The gun barked again, and a ragged hole appeared in Boadie's right hand where his fore finger knuckle had been. That second round skated across Boadie's forehead and continued south down Homan Avenue.

"Fat Boo, watch out!" Shameka screamed.

Boadie looked beyond Fat Boo and saw that there were several young men running down the side walk on the other side of the street with guns in their hands. Fat Boo turned and opened fire on the gunmen, taking cover beside his SUV. The gunmen shot back, and the rapid drum of fully-automatic gunfire frightened Boadie into lying flat on his back in the middle of the salted-down sidewalk. He heard glass shattering. He heard Shameka's horrified screams. A stray bullet slammed into his left leg, just below the kneecap. A puff of snow exploded next to his bleeding face. A passing Buick Sedan braked and lost traction, slamming into the front-end of Fat Boo's SUV.

Through chattering teeth, Boadie found the strength to mutter a single word: "M-M-Markio."

***

Lil James and his 22-year-old brother—Jay-Jay—stepped out into the street, shooting their guns at Fat Boo's X6, while Trav, Ceno, Lud Foe and three others shot their guns from the sidewalk. The barrage of rapid gunfire racked the BMW on its wheels, even as Fat Boo reached over the hood and shot back. The Buick that had crashed into the BMW belonged to Alayna Duncan, a fat, pretty girl whose sister was Raven, one of the baddest strippers at Redbone's. Lil James could see Alayna and her boyfriend—Drayshon— ducking low in their seats as the bullets flew over their heads.

Lil James had seen Fat Boo standing next to Boadie the moment he walked out of Buck's front door, but he hadn't realized that there was a gun involved until he heard the first gunshot, and he'd immediately drawn his 9-millimeter Kel-Tec pistol.

"I'm finna nail this fat-ass nigga," he muttered to himself as he and Jay-Jay started across to Fat Boo's side of the street.

They'd only made it halfway across Homan Avenue when a black Escalade slid to a stop at the 16th Street intersection. The doors flew open, and three ski-masked men bailed out with their Glocks blowing, cutting down Lil James and his brother almost instantly.

Lil James was the lucky one. He caught five bullets—two to the stomach, one in the hip, and two more through his left thigh. He went down hard, taking aim at the three masked men and squeezing off half a dozen shots in their direction.

His brother, Jay-Jay, wasn't so lucky. He'd only suffered one gunshot wound, but the bullet had entered through the top of his right ear and left a gaping hole in the left side of his head, divorcing two fat dreadlocks from his scalp and sending them flying through the air in a crimson mist of blood, cranial bone, and brain matter.

Lil James was dragging himself toward his brother's unmoving body, impervious to the steady clap of gunfire all around him, when a white-and-blue CPD Tahoe came skidding off of 15th street. The flashing lights triggered everyone to flee, and the gang that had been gathered inside Buck's house began piling into the vehicles they'd arrived in—two Dodge Challengers, two Chargers, and a Durango, all of them with Hellcat engines that pretty much guaranteed a fast getaway.

Two white policemen jumped out of the Tahoe. One of them yelled, "Freeze! CPD! Drop the fucking weapons!" And then they both started shooting, firing at the three masked gunmen as they loaded Fat Boo into the Escalade and raced away, heading west down 16th Street.

Lud Foe's silenced Mac-11 came out the rear driver's side window of his Challenger and sprayed the two cops with 9-millimeter rounds as his tires spun out on the snow slick street, and suddenly there were four wounded men stretched out in the street, and three others bleeding from multiple bullet wounds on the sidewalk.

But the only wounded man Lil James was worried about was his little brother, who had died instantly—just like one of the policemen.

Chapter 6

"So, what do you think?" Karim Caruthers asked, the confident smile of his coffee-brown visage showing that he already knew the answer to the question.

Seated next to Nikkia on the opposite side of the gold-bottomed coffee table, Markio wore a smile that spanned the entire width of his face. He flipped to the next page and kept reading.

This was the real reason Nikkia had brought him down to Miami Beach. She'd paid Karim Caruthers—an Oscar-winning Hollywood film director/screenwriter—a quarter of a million dollars to write the screenplay for the Bird Man, Markio's best selling debut novel, and it was everything he'd hoped it would be.

"I like it," Markio said. Which was an understatement. He loved it.

'I've applied for all the necessary filming permits from the city of Chicago. They should be approved within the next couple of weeks. I don't expect any problems. We should be able to start filming by May."

Markio was beyond elated. His iPhones were buzzing like crazy in his pocket, but those calls would have to wait. This was his dream. He'd envisioned his novels as movies from the very start, sitting in his cramped little prison cell with nothing more than a Bic ink pen and pack of writing paper, and now Nikkia had gone behind his back to bring his dream to fruition.

He turned to her and kissed her on the mouth. Once, twice, thrice—three wet, passionate kisses that left her glowing as she sat next to him on the sumptuous Italian leather Versace sofa. Standing beside the glass-topped coffee table (the base of which was a Medusa head made of gold, with the snakes holding up the glass), Alexus was smiling even harder than Nikkia.

"I'll finance the whole thing," Alexus said. "Whatever it costs. I'll even make an appearance in the film if you need me to, make my acting debut. Whatever it takes to make this movie a huge success. You're one of my favorite authors. I want to see you succeed."

"I don't know what to say." Markio shook his head in disbelief. He thought the screenplay had been geniusly written. Karim had truly outdone himself. From *Fade in* to *Fade out*, each scene depicted the story just as Markio had written it. It was no wonder Caruthers was such a highly acclaimed screenwriter.

Markio looked around the spacious sitting room, wishing his cousins could be here with him. They had left out with Leon and Mike to explore the beaches and do a little shopping. Kay wanted to be the freshest street nigga in the club tonight. "Gotta put on for the city," he'd said on the FaceTime call with Markio just twenty minutes ago.

"I've already spoken with Jamie," Karim said, getting up from the U-shaped sofa, which surrounded the Medusa table on three sides. "He's interested. Taraj's interested. We'll do a table reading and see who all shows up. Since COVID hit, the majority of the actors I know have been auditioning over Zoom. I'll email the script to a few others and see if they're interested. I know one thing for certain: once word gets out that Alexus is in on this, all of Black Hollywood will be competing for a role in the film. They'll be beating down my door."

"I appreciate you, man." Markio stood and reached across the table to shake Karim's hand. The man had a firm, professional grasp, though his palm felt a bit sweaty. His face was pock-marked, like Seal's. His impeccable three-piece suit was navy-blue and expensive looking.

Markio and Nikkia trailed Karim and Alexus (and four of Alexus's brawny bodyguards) to the foyer. As they waved goodbye to Karim, Markio closed his lean arms around Nikkio's waist and pulled her close, loving the softness of her ass against the front of his pants. Smooching at the nape of her neck, he whispered, "I love you, woman. I'm dead serious. Thanks."

He could see the smirk on the side of her sexy face as she gave the back of his hand an affectionate squeeze. He kissed the ball of her shoulder. Hugged her tighter.

Alexus turned to look at them, rolled her eyes, and smilingly said, "Ain't nobody tryna see all that." She glanced at her glistening diamond watch and added, "I have a couple of phone calls to make. The federal police in Culiacan, Sinaloa just arrested Ovidio Gozman, one of El Chapo's sons. There's going to be hell to pay. Kia, I'll text you in a few."

Alexus headed off in the direction of Bullet Face's studio, and Markio went up the stairs behind Nikkia, biting and planting kisses all over her backside as they went.

"Boy, will you stop?" Nikkia laughed, swatting a hand behind her.

But Markio didn't stop. He kept kissing on her soft buttocks, going from cheek to cheek, ignoring the incessantly ringing iPhone in his pocket. He was floating on cloud nine, and he wasn't about to let anyone bring him back down to earth.

He scooped Nikkia up and threw her over his shoulder, smiling widely as she laughed merrily, smacking her on the ass as she playfully pounded on his back.

"Boy, if you don't put me down," she said, her legs flailing wildly in the air.

Markio ignored her request yet again, keeping her on his shoulder and carrying her into the bedroom she'd selected for them to stay in. It was by far the most elegant bedroom Markio had ever seen, even more opulent than the Four Seasons honeymoon suite they spent the night in last summer. Everything, from the rugs and drapes, to the bedding and lamp shades, was Versace, black with gold embroidering, which seemed to be the prevailing color scheme of nearly every room in the mansion. The adjoining bathroom had two sinks sunken into a white marble countertop, a glassed-in-shower with a glass bench and a large smart TV embedded in the marble wall, and two toilets flanking a claw foot bathtub spacious enough to bathe two adults at once.

Markio dumped Nikkia onto the bed and went to shut and lock the door.

"You should rethink this whole Whitney situation," Nikkia said, sitting up and smiling gloriously. "I mean, we already told her we're coming. It would be so rude of us to back out on her over a petty little argument. She already feels like I stole you from her. I'd hate to make it worse by ditching her grand opening. She'd never forgive me for that."

"Fuck that bitch." Markio removed his shirt and undid the Velcro straps on his bullet-proof vest. "I don't even wanna hear her name no more. Take them clothes off."

Nikkia's pretty mouth fell open in mock horror. "How dare you speak so vulgarly to me. I am a woman. You cannot speak to me this way."

An amused chuckle tumbled out of Markio's throat. He draped his shirt and vest over the arm of a heavy leather armchair, nodding slowly and thoughtfully.

"Okay," he said. "I see how we gon' play this."

His mind was set on becoming aggressive, but Nikkia folded before he got the chance to rip off her sexy Ivy Park bodysuit. Biting down on her lower lip, she undressed hurriedly, until she was only wearing a tan-lace Savage X Fenty bra-and-thong set and her glistening diamond jewelry.

"I know one thing," she said, wiggling her flawlessly pedicured toes. "I'd better be making a cameo appearance in that movie. If not, you can forget about a sequel."

Markio almost threw back his head and howled; he was so happy. His book series was actually going to be movie! He'd recently lain in bed with Nikkia and watched the *True to the Game* movies, all three of them, and he'd constantly found himself daydreaming about how exciting it would be to have his own novels adapted to a screenplay (or, God willing, multiple screenplays). He'd read Terri Woods' *True to the Game* series way back when he was a teen, and it had been great to see all those memorable characters brought to life.

Now the same thing was about to happen to the novels he'd written, and it was all because of his stunningly attractive girlfriend—Nikkia Staples—who was now sitting at the edge of the California King bed, her thick ass and thighs spread out beneath her slim waistline like a Thanksgiving buffet.

"I'm about to break my dick in your guts," Markio said, walking toward her.

"Fine by me," she replied. "As long as you break that tongue first."

***

The ground began to vibrate as Tyquan Holton's candy-printed money-green GMC Yukon Denali XL swerved into the gas station. It was the SUV's thunderous sound system that made the earth shake: six twelve-inch speakers and two powerful amplifiers that had cost Tyquan almost ten thousand dollars. The Denali rode on gold 30-inch Forgiato rims, and its windows were so darkly tinted that you had to peer in through the windshield to get a look at the passengers.

Flocka watched the Denali pull in from the passenger's seat of his friend Lil Jimmy's canary yellow Camaro, which was idling at pump number two. Lil Jimmy was inside the gas station, flirting with Dejane, the sexy young store clerk. Flocka's girlfriend—Jimmy's seventeen-year-old sister Ava—was mean-mugging him through the screen of his iPhone, but the sound of the approaching Denali had taken his attention off the FaceTime call.

The sight of the flashy green Denali made Flocka's blood boil.

Up until six months ago, Tyquan had been a real-deal lame, laughed at by just about everyone who knew him. When Tyquan and Flocka's cousin—Benji—were robbed at gunpoint outside of Tyquan's ex-girlfriend's apartment, an eyewitness to the robbery had recorded a video of Tyquan pissing his pants while kneeling before one of the gunmen. The video had gone viral on social media, making Tyquan the laughing stock of town.

But a few hours after the robbery, thanks to Flocka and Benji, Tyquan was able to redeem himself when the three of them shot and killed two Chicago men—Emmanuel Parker and Herman Patterson Jr.—who'd been trying to break into the two flats where Tyquan had lived with his mother—Taquisha—and his grandmother: Miss Jeanetta. Tyquan's uncle—Markio—had warned them of the robbery plot, and they'd been prepared and waiting. The shooting had taken place at a time when bodies were dropping left and right, and the fact that they'd gotten off on self-defense, and that Tyquan had taken a bullet to the gut during the shootout, had made the three of them the most popular young niggas in Michigan City.

Then things had changed soon after Tyquan was released from the hospital. He sold the fourteen pounds of exotic weed Markio had given him shortly before the shooting to a Gangster Disciple named Straw for $4,500-a-pound. On top of that, just three days later, Markio blessed him with

$75,000 in cash and another fifty pounds of some even better weed. Feeling himself, Tyquan had dumped his girlfriend for a bad bitch named Taliah from Flint, Michigan. He'd bought the Denali and put it in the shop for upgrades while he drove around town in a Mercedes rental. He'd moved out of his mother's apartment to some unknown out-of-town address and changed his phone number, telling everyone to just hit him up through social media, and since then he'd started flossing on Instagram in all the latest designer gear, smoking fat blunts of the very best weed and flashing huge piles of cash, allowing his followers a glimpse of the Caribbean vacations and shopping trips he and Taliah took to Atlanta's swanky Buckhead Village.

The lifestyle upgrades wouldn't have bothered Flocka had he remained a part of it all. But that wasn't the case. Tyquan had ditched both Flocka and Benji. He'd ditched the two loyal friends who'd likely saved his life. That was what had Flocka's blood boiling. Tyquan was balling out of control while Flocka and Benji were struggling to get by. Sure, Tyquan had blessed Flocka and Benji with a pound of Black Cherry Gelato each, and he'd bought them some Jordan sneakers and stuffed $1,000 in each shoe, but that was small change. Just last week, Loachie, one of Flocka's fellow GDs, had bought four pounds of Black Cherry Gelato from Tyquan for $24,000. Another GD called Dog Head had bought seven pounds from Tyquan that same day. Flocka knew all this because Tyquan had been bragging to Eva—Ava's identical twin sister—and Eva told Flocka everything.

"You need to stay away from my twin," Ava was saying. "You're getting too close with her, and I don't like it. That bitch is sneaky, and she's crazy, and I wouldn't be at all surprised if she tried to sneak around with you behind my back."

"You trippin', baby," Flocka said without looking at the smart phone in his hand. His eyes were on the Denali, waiting to see Tyquan emerge from inside it.

"I ain't trippin'! You and her text more than we do. That's not normal, Flocka. It's weird, it gets under my skin, and I want it to stop."

The passenger's door of the Denali swung open, and Tyquan stepped out of it dressed in a white leather Amiri jacket over blue designer jeans and light blue Timberland boots. His pockets were bulging, and he was all smiles, showing off the sixteen VVS diamond teeth he'd revealed on Instagram just yesterday. An extended magazine stuck straight out in front of him from the butt of the Glock in the holster under his arm. Taliah was in the driver's seat, laughing with Tyquan about something while she dug around in her large Louis Vuitton purse.

Flocka clenched and gritted his teeth as he watched Tyquan push his door shut and walk toward the gas station glass front doors. Tyquan glanced into Lil Jimmy's car and gave Flocka an enthusiastic nod. Flocka smirked and returned the gesture, albeit a bit coldly.

"You're not even paying attention to me," Ava complained bitterly. Two seconds later, she sucked her teeth and ended the call.

Flocka's infuriated gaze landed on his phone screen half a second before Ava's gorgeous face disappeared. She and her twin sister Eva were two of the baddest bitches this small city of thirty-five-thousand had to offer. They were redbones, and their bodies were just as flawless and thickly proportioned as their mother's. Unbeknown to Ava, Flocka had already fucked both Eva and their heartachingly attractive yellowbone of a mother—Whitney Clarrett—and now he had his sights set on Joselyn, their equally beautiful fifteen-year-old sister.

Reluctantly, he called Ava back, preparing himself for the fiery exchange of words that was certain to come. But to his surprise, the face that popped up on his phone screen didn't belong to Ava. It was her mother, Whitney Clarrett, and Whitney did not look happy.

There was a single palm tree swaying in the breeze behind Whitney's head. Flocka knew that all three of her sexy teenage daughters had flown down to Miami for the much anticipated grand opening of *iKiss Kosmetics*, and he wondered what the weather was like down there. Here in Michigan City, Indiana, the temperature had risen to an unseasonably warm thirty-nine degrees—chilly, but nowhere near as frigid as it usually was this time of year.

"I need your help again," Whitney said. The last time she'd asked for his help, she'd had him and his friend Melvo break into a house Markio had just moved into; Melvo had ended up dead, his brains spattered all over the back porch, and Flocka had ended up in jail.

"Awww shit," he said warily. "What you need me to do this time?"

"It's Markio again, I never told you this before, but you know those eight suitcases I wanted you to take from Markio's house that day?"

Flocka nodded. The suitcases were what he and Melvo had searched every room in Markio's house for that day. Whitney had offered him $50,000 to retrieve the suitcases, and since he hadn't found them, she'd only given him five grand.

"Well," she explained, "Markio had five million dollars in those suitcases, and he was supposed to split with me. He only gave me fifty thousand dollars. That's why I had y'all break in his house to try and find the suitcases."

Flocka tilted his head to one side and regarded Whitney with a questioning squint. A flurry of thoughts swirled through his head: So Markio had $5 million in those suitcases, and this bitch only offered me $50,000? What kinda fuck-nigga she think I am?

"I know what you're thinking," Whitney said. "And you're right I should have told you. It was all new to me at the time, and I just wasn't thinking straight. I wasn't even sure if he had five million dollars. He had lied and told me it was way less."

Flocka looked up as a dark blue Ford Focus pulled up to the front of the gas station and parked. Three pretty Black girls climbed out of it. One of them was Ashley Murry, AKA "Amazing Ashley," a tall, thick nineteen-year-old from Indianapolis. Flocka had been after her for months, but all he'd managed to get out of her was a single nude video of her bouncing ass. She and her two friends stared in through the building's front windows, all of them seemingly excited to see Tyquan.

"But anyway," Whitney went on, "he's playing me really hard right now, and I'm pissed about it. I've been talking to Nissa. She said Markio's been flooding the streets with zah. Black-ass Reggie and Tyquan are selling it for him. They've been vacuum-sealing it and shipping it out through the mail for months now. Nissa's brother—Cortez—bought sixty pounds of Gelato, and they mailed it straight to his girl's house in Memphis."

"That bitch-ass nigga Tyquan right here." Flocka switched to the rear-facing camera and raised his iPhone so Whitney could see Tyquan who was standing at the open glass door of a beverage cooler, taking out a 20-ounce bottle of Sprite while Amazon Ashley and her two friends snapped photos of him and selfies with him in the background. Irritated by the attention Tyquan was receiving—particularly from Amazon Ashley—Flocka quickly switched back to the front facing camera. "They actin'like this nigga a celebrity or some'n."

"It's probably because they know he's Markio's nephew," Whitney surmised. "Alexus just posted a pic with Markio on IG and people are already losing their minds over it."

Flocka's thick eyebrows came together. "Alexus? You mean *Alexus*?"

"Yes, I mean *Alexus*. The billionaire. He's at the Versace Mansion with her as we speak. That picture she just posted will probably get him three or four million new book sales, and his shady-ass girlfriend is worth two hundred million dollars, yet he can't give me the two-point five million he owes me. The shit is really pissing me off."

A savage scowl lifted one corner of Flocka's top lip. Now he was even more envious of Tyquan. Here, Flocka was sitting in the passenger's seat of his best friends Camaro like a certified scrub, while Tyquan and his uncle were winning harder than ever.

"So," Flocka asked through clenched teeth, "what you need me to do?"

"I need you to find out where Tyquan lives. Or Reggie— either one is fine with me. I'll be flying in with my boyfriend and a few of his guys tomorrow night. All we need is an address."

"I don't know where neither of them live. I know Tyquan stay out of town somewhere but that's it. I barely even know Reggie."

Whitney went silent for a long moment; then: "My sister Candace has two of those AirTags, the GPS trackers her girlfriend bought her for Christmas. I'll have her bring you one just stick it to Tyquan's truck, and I'll track it to wherever he lives. And this time, I promise, I'll give you a whole lot more than five thousand dollars. Even if I have to pay you out of my own pocket."

* * *

Nikkia Staples had an exceptionally pretty pussy. The lips were fat and silky, the clitoris a pink little nub tucked inside its hood; every time she spread the lips apart, Markio was amazed by how wet the pink inner walls always were.

This time, just as he'd done the last time and a hundred times before that, he ran the flat of his tongue between the meaty folds of her labia and up to her hooded clitoris, where he paused to suck and lick and inhale the captivating scent of her juicy womanhood.

Nikkia tilted her head back and breathed in deeply. A few seconds later, a low moan escaped her open mouth, and she arched her back. Markio's tongue moved as smoothly and expertly as a trained ballet dancer, flickering across her sensitive clit, and up and down her swollen vaginal lips.

Sunlight spilled into the room through two tall windows; a Mexican maid had tied back the black-and-gold Versace drapes. *Avatar: The Way of Water* was playing on the 120-inch smart TV. Dust motes twirled through the air, illuminated by the rays of sunshine.

But the only thing Nikkia could focus on at the moment was the titillating feeling of Markio's tongue roaming across her most erogenous region. He massaged her thighs and squeezed her breasts as he sucked on her pussy. He made slurping sounds on her clitoris and slipped two fingers inside of her to rub on her G-spot. Which sent her to bucking and moaning, until finally she seized up and came all over his probing fingers.

"Yeah," Markio said, nodding triumphantly as he rose up onto his knees. His wet mouth formed an arrogant little smirk. "You know what time it is. It's Mr. Nasty time."

Nikkia laughed out loud and tried to shove him away, but he already had his nearly eleven-inch-long erection jutting out over his designer boxers, guiding it toward her slippery opening. She gasped as the head dipped into her, and then the rest of his intimidating length slid in behind it, causing her delicate vaginal walls to expand as his fat black snake filled her to capacity. He lifted her legs and pushed them toward her head, folding her in half. He leaned in and kissed her on the mouth, and she tasted herself on his lips.

"I hope you know how much I really love you, Nikkia," he said, and pressed into her, closing one strong hand around the front of her neck and squeezing. "You changed my life, made me a better man. You bought me a fuckin' Rolls Royce, got me a movie deal. I'll never forget that shit." He slid halfway out of her and slammed forward again; she yelped, and her pussy made a wet, slashing sound. "That's why Ima fuck the dog shit outta you every chance I get."

And with that said, he began to fuck the dog shit out of her, leaning back a little and pounding in and out of her tight little pussy until she was creaming all over his lengthy black pole. She wrapped her arms around the back of her knees and held her legs back, her moans becoming loud and lascivious screams as Markio penetrated her again and again.

She heard footfalls passing by outside the bedroom door. Both of Markio's iPhones were ringing incessantly in the pocket of his Dior sweatpants, which lay in a crumpled head on the floor. He'd gone deaf to every discernible interruption, far too enthralled by the sight of his own dick plunging into Nikkia's creamy center to care about anything else.

Which suited Nikkia just fine. This was the kind of sex she'd always wanted from a partner. Great dick and even better head. A man who could give Nikkia those two things could get anything out of her. Her ex-husband's sex game had been weak—mediocre head and a five-inch erection—but she'd stuck it out with him for almost twenty years. And for what? She didn't have a clue aside from the unnerving thought of her boys growing up in a single-parent home.

Now that she was with Markio, she realized what she'd been missing and needing all along—some of that good street-nigga dick, the kind of dick that didn't slow the strokes when tears welled up in her eyes, the kind of dick that touched her very soul and left her pussy bruised and swollen for days on end. That was the kind of dick Markio served her on a daily basis, and he never let her forget it.

"Bitch, I'm Millionaire Markio," he muttered, leaning in to choke her again. "You better put some respect on this dick, you hear me? Hm? Hm?"

Nikkia gave a subtle nod. She could feel the veins bulging out of her forehead from a lack of oxygen. Markio loosened his grip on her neck, and as her lips parted to suck in a much-needed breath air, he spat right down into her gaping mouth and began kissing her lips, sucking them, and she clawed at his back. His impetuously thrusting dick hadn't been in her five minutes when she tensed and trembled through a second orgasm that felt at least twice as intense as the first.

She shoved away from him again, and this time she pushed hard enough to dislodge his pistoning erection from her quivering vagina. She scurried sideways and fell off the side of the bed, landing on her back on an ultra-soft Versace area rug. She began to laugh, breathlessly and shakily.

"Oh, my God," she said between breaths. "Shit. Wait. Wait a minute."

But Markio didn't wait three seconds. He stepped down from the bed, his Cuban-link necklaces clinking noisily on his well-built chest, his oversized appendage sticking out in front of him like the arm of some muscle-bound toddler. He went to his knees on the rug, lifted Nikkia's legs onto his shoulders, and gently eased his dick right back inside of her.

"Are you trying to kill me in here?" Nikkia asked jokingly.

Her joking expression faded away rather quickly as Markio started pounding in and out of her again. "Shut up," he whispered next to her ear. He kissed and scrapped his teeth against the side of her neck. "Shut the fuck up."

Nikkia tried to keep quiet, but she couldn't get her mouth to shut, and the high-pitched, yelping moans kept bursting out of her. She dug her fingernails into Markio's lower back, and her eyes rolled up in their sockets, as if she'd acquired an evil spirit that necessitated an exorcism. Three of her toe knuckles popped as her neatly pedicured toes curled over. Her upper and lower jaw separated, stretching her mouth open wider than the mouth on the *Scream* mask. It felt like someone was literally reaching up into her pussy and punching her insides with a closed fist—a painful feeling, but an undeniably good feeling.

"Oooouuu," she moaned ceaselessly, wanting it to end, wanting it to never end.

"Yeah," Markio said cockily. "I told you. Didn't I tell you? I told yo' ass, you better…put some motha…fuckin' respect on this dick."

"I respect it," Nikkia cried, as a single tear trickled down from her left eye and became lost somewhere in her sew-in.

Twenty or thirty minutes passed by; Nikkia wasn't sure of the exact duration of time. It was difficult keeping track of time when she was getting the soul fucked right of her body. She was only vaguely aware of Markio picking her up from the rug and bending her over the side of the bed, and then he was fucking her again, his strong veiny brown hands caressing her hips and ass, his chains making metallic clinking noises, the blue people on the enormous TV screen riding their otherworldly sea creatures through the water. Nikkia had really wanted to watch the new Avatar movie, but now it was the furthest thing from her mind.

She rested the side of her sexy face on the heavy Versace comforter and balled her hands into tight fists, allowing the recurrent *smack-smack-smack* of Markio's chiseled abdomen against her wobbling ass to relax her mind. This was heaven; she decided if and when she ever died, she hoped to God that this exact moment would repeat itself for all eternity.

Ten minutes later, a third orgasm swept through Nikkia, this bringing tiny white dots into her vision and causing her legs to shake and wobble uncontrollably. And then Markio clamped his hands onto her waist and dug in deep, and she could feel his dick spasming within the contracting walls of her pussy, spewing an overflow of semen inside of her. It was like in the movies: they were actually climaxing together, simultaneously.

Afterward, depleted of both strength and breath, the two of them climbed into bed and inserted themselves between the covers. Nikkia chuckled aloud as she rested her jaw on Markio's chest, using the painted nail of one forefinger to trace the *Chicago Bulls* logo he had inked onto his left pectoral muscle.

"The fuck is you laughin' at?" Markio asked weakly.

"Ohhh, nothing." Nikkia shut her eyes and breathed a sigh of great relief. "Just hoping you didn't break my vagina, because that's what it feels like."

"You'll be a'ight," Markio said, and he dozed off eight seconds later.

Meanwhile, on the floor near the foot of the bed, buried behind a fifty-thousand-dollar bundle of hundred-dollar bills in the right-hand pocket of his Dior joggers, his two iPhones had yet to stop ringing.

Chapter 7

It had been over four hours since CPD Officer Richard Westman was shot and killed at the corner of 15th Street and Homan Avenue.

Since then, the Chicago Police Department had sectioned off Homan Avenue from 16th Street to Douglas Boulevard. News vans from all the local stations—NBC5, ABC7, Fox32, and MTN22—were parked just beyond the yellow tape, their field reporters standing out in the cold, reposting live from the scene of the city's latest mass shooting.

The police had already arrested fourteen reputed members of the Traveling Vice Lords and 4 Corner Hustlers, several of whom had not even been in the area when the deadly mid-day shootout took place. Trav of Sicko Mobb was arrested simply because a traffic camera had captured his car speeding off down 16th Street shortly after the shooting. Cocky Lord, a high-ranking TVL who also happened to be one of Markio's close friends, was pulled over leaving his Homan Avenue residence and busted with a backpack full of cash and an AR-15 assault rifle with an attached bump stock that made it fire like a fully-automatic weapon.

In all, well over two hundred spent shell casings were found on Homan Avenue in the aftermath of the shooting, which had left four dead (including an 82-year-old grandfather who was shot through his living room window) and nine others wounded.

Tammy watched it all play out from the safety of her comfortable living room sofa. She was curled up beneath an old quilted blanket with a mug of hot cocoa in one hand and her smart phone in the other, listening to Fox 32 News coverage of the shooting on her 50-inch Roku TV while she scrolled through Facebook, viewing all the posts about the deadly broad-day shootout.

Daija, a pretty chocolate girl Tammy had gone to school with, had posted a video of Cocky Lord's arrest. The police had ripped him from the driver's seat of his red Jeep Wagoneer and slammed him violently onto the hood of their patrol car. Someone else had posted several videos of the shooting scene, showing Lil James and Jay Jay as they lay shot up in the street, and Binky's baby mama Shamaeka—shot up and slumped sideways in Fat Boo's X6. And the two policemen, the one shot through the knee attempting to save the life of the one who'd taken a bullet through the eye. Someone in a gray Chevy Lumina had helped Boadie into their car and rushed him to a nearby hospital; Tammy had seen the Lumina around the neighborhood, but she couldn't remember who owned it.

"Markio is going to lose his mind over this shit," Tammy murmured, shaking her head.

Her older cousin—Big Jessica—gave her a questioning glance from the opposite end of the faux leather sofa; Big J had her smart phone to her ear, talking to Rock, the baby-daddy of hers who was currently serving out an eighteen-year sentence for voluntary manslaughter at Lawrence Correctional Center. He'd shot and killed Danny Lord, Big J's other baby-daddy.

Tammy got up and went to the kitchen to check on the steaks she had slow-roasting in the oven. Her string beans and mac-and-cheese were already done, and she'd bought two German chocolate cakes for dessert. She could hear her daughter—Tanyjah "Ny-Ny" Maxwell—laughing and talking with her cousins—Wendy and Raquelle, who were

Big J's two daughters. If there was one honest statement that could be made about Tammy, it was that she truly did love and adore her seven-year-old daughter. She may have had a promiscuous reputation in the streets, but she used the money she got from the men she slept with to take good care of Tanyjah. Ny-Ny got everything she wanted. Her Christmas list had totaled almost twenty-four hundred dollars, and Tammy had given her men hell until she had every gift wrapped and piled beneath the tree that still stood in one corner of her living room.

Which made Tammy think of the $20,000 Markio's sister Shakia had brought to her front door less than an hour ago. Tammy had stuffed the cash down into the front of her jeans to keep Big J from seeing it, and she' shut the door on Shakia rather abruptly. Afterward, she'd slipped into her bedroom and stashed the bundle of hundreds under her mattress.

Now, as she pushed the oven door shut, she thought about all the other things she could do for her daughter with $20,000 at her disposal. First and foremost, she'd be able to relocate to a safer neighborhood, something she'd been wanting to do for years. Her childhood friend—Kiara—lived in Houston, and she was always telling Tammy how nice it was down there. "I'd move down to Texas in a heartbeat if I could," Tammy had said during their last FaceTime conversation. "I just ain't got the money right now."

Well, now she did have the money. And if she followed through with Markio's plan to set up Esco, she'd have an additional $50,000 to go along with the twenty grand she had under her mattress. That kind of money could go a long way. Seventy thousand dollars was more than enough to put a hefty down payment on a nice quarter-million-dollar home, and she'd also have the extras to start her very own business. Ny-Ny would be in a more promising school district, affording her the opportunity to become a more well-rounded human being and, hopefully, a successful young woman later on in life. And for sure there would be an untapped pool of local middle class men, all of them ripe for the picking. Tammy's lifelong dream of one day being married to a handsome, successful black man had a much better chance of becoming a reality in a region where no one knew of her promiscuities.

These were among he many reasons why Tammy had canceled her dick appointment with Jock and replaced him with Esco. She'd texted Jock not even five minutes after Markio's sister delivered the $20,000: '*Jock, I'm so sorry, but Big J brought her kids over here and she got an emergency going on with her baby daddy. Can we link tomorrow night instead?*'

Jock had messaged back with a thumbs-up emoji, and minutes later he'd gone live on Instagram from a party at the house of Tammy's old friend—Miesha Lynwood—in K-Town. Miesha was all over him in the video, twerking her big fake ass against the front of his jeans, and suddenly Tammy was glad she'd turned him down. She knew for a fact that Miesha had herpes, and she didn't want anything to do with anyone Miesha was fucking.

Tammy went back to her living room and stood looking out the window, first studying the spot where Binky was killed earlier in the day and then sweeping her attentive gaze west down Douglas, searching for Esco's car. The street was dark, lit only by apartment windows, street lights, and headlights—and also, from somewhere further down Douglas Boulevard, the foreboding blue-red flash of police lights.

She was still looking out the window when Big J ended the call with Rock and connected her smart phone to the phone charger they'd been sharing all day.

"So, what's up with Rock?" Tammy asked, for the sake of conversation.

"Same shit. Gangbangin' in prison like he don't wanna come home." Big J took a pint of Hennessy out of her purse and spun the top loose. "He had already heard about Binky and Jay Jay gettin' killed. His cellie's cousin used to be married to Binky's auntie, or something like that. Anyway, he say all they been talkin' about is Markio and that lawyer he's engaged to. I can't remember her name."

"It's Nikkia. Nikkia Staples. And they're not engaged." Tammy consulted her iPhone for clarification, just in case Nikkia or Markio had posted anything about an engagement since the last time she'd checked their pages an hour ago. They hadn't. Nikkia's last post was a video of herself posing in a mirror; Markio's was a video from his last book signing.

"Well, whatever they are, that lil nigga is smart as shit," Big J said, "I was just on the phone with his sister Taquisha before I got over here. She said her phone ain't stopped blowin' up ever since Alexus Castilla posted that picture with Markio. Everybody and they mama been callin' her."

Tammy's eyes lit up, and her thumbs worked at record speed, bringing up one of the most followed pages on Instagram *@TheAlexusCastilla;* it was currently at 402.8 million followers. The only female celebrity whose follower count even came close to hers was Kylie Jenner.

The photo of Markio and Alexus was the last one Alexus had posted to her page, her first post in weeks. Alexus was stunning as usual in a white-sequined mini-dress that likely cost more than everything Tammy owned, her lashy green eyes and luscious-lipped smile as breathtaking as ever, and standing next to her was Markio Earl. He looked like a rap star in all his diamond jewelry and Dior apparel.

"Okay," Tammy said decidedly, "now I have to fuck this nigga. His ass is about to be famous Fay-mous. Oh, my God. I wonder if Bullet Face was there."

She double-tapped the photo, which had already racked up more than four million likes. Scrolling through the comments, she saw that many of Alexus's followers wanted to know the identity of the man with whom she was standing.

Tammy turned away from the window and stared at Jessica Brandley, the older cousin she'd been looking up to ever since she was a toddler. But J was more of a sister than a cousin. They'd gone through a thousand ups and a million downs together, and the bond they shared had only grown stronger.

"That man is in a whole committed relationship," Big J said, her nicotine-stained teeth on full display as she smiled at her pint of cognac. "I've known Markio since he was a lil bitty kid, fightin' all the other kids on Trumbull. You might've had a chance with him before he went to prison, but now?" She shook her dark-complected head, and her ponytail swayed with the movement. "He's a man now, Tammy. A real man. He got himself a good woman who takes good care of him. He wouldn't cheat on that girl with Rihanna."

Tammy hardly even heard her big cousin's advice; she was still salivating over the photo. Markio was short like Yo Gotti, Tammy's all-time favorite gangsta rapper, and he had a cold aura about him, an aura that seemed to say *I'm a cool guy, but if you play with me I'll fucking kill you.*

A sweep of headlights across her living room windows snatched Tammy's attention away from the photo. She looked outside and saw Esco's blood-red Challenger circling around from the eastbound lane on Douglas Boulevard to the westbound land, parking two spaces in front of her Charger.

She backed away from the window and texted the number Markio had given her earlier. '*Esco just pulled up to my apartment. I'm about to sit in the car with him for a second. Make sure if you send somebody they don't hit me.*'

The message was read almost instantly, but there were no undulating dots that showed Markio was texting a reply. Three seconds later, Tammy answered an incoming FaceTime call from Esco.

"I'm out here," he said gruffly.

Tammy put on her most seductive smile. "Okay. I'll be right down."

***

Esco was six feet tall, a powerfully built man who had clearly done a lot of weight lifting in prison. About fifteen or twenty braids criss-crossed his light-brown scalp, each braid ending with a red rubber band. His hairline was as straight as a razor's edge. He wore a red Givenchy sweater over designer jeans and red-and-black Nike Air Maxes, and Tammy thought he smelled amazing as she joined him in the back seat of his Challenger.

He had two of his boys with him. Po Boy and Lil Devin. They were in the front seats, sipping liquor from red plastic solo cups. Both of them were young, in their late teens or early twenties, and they both wore their hair in long dreadlocks. Po Boy, the chubbier of the two, had a fat pile of twenty-dollar bills in one hand and a pistol with an extended clip on his lap. This was an up and coming money team; Tammy, a professional gold digger, could sense these things. She knew when a clique was serious about getting money and when they were merely in the way. Esco had his gang focused on securing the bag.

"Why am I getting in the back seat?" Tammy asked as she got in beside Esco.

"It's dangerous out here. Gotta keep my security with me," Esco replied, turning up his bottle of Miller Genuine Draft beer.

Tammy showed a nervous smile. She had initiated a highly sexual conversation with Esco over Facebook Messenger, just to see if he was gullible enough to fall for such a move, and unsurprisingly he'd fallen right into her thirst trap, hook, line, and sinker. She'd said she would suck his dick for an hour if he came over tonight; he'd sent her a video detailing the ways he would suck and lick on her pussy while she sucked him off, and how far he'd dig his tongue into her asshole. The idea of receiving that kind of head had dampened the crotch of her booty shorts, and she'd taken a nice long moment in the shower with her rose vibrator to relieve the sexual tension.

She'd asked Esco to bring her some Percocet pills. He produced a Tylenol bottle from his pocket and dumped two thirty-milligram Percs into the palm of her hand. She popped one and pocketed the other one for Big J. Esco handed her his beer, and even though she had already swallowed the pill, she chased it down with a large gulp of the cold malt liquor.

"Who all you got up there?" Esco asked, leaning across her lap to peer up at her apartment windows.

"Just my big cousin Jessica and our kids. Ain't nobody in my bedroom. We can go in there and turn up the music for a lil while."

Easing back over to his side of the back seat, Esco slipped the thick fingers of one strong, battle-scarred hand between Tammy's closed legs and pressed his fingertips against the crotch of the skin-tight sweat pants she'd thrown on after her shower. The sweats were red, like her Pelle jacket, like Esco's high-end designer outfit and the exterior paint on his Challenger. He leaned in and whispered in her ear.

"You washed that pussy like I told you to?"

Simpering, Tammy nodded. The four of them shifted their attention to a police car that was cruising in their direction on the opposite side of the promenade that spanned the length of Douglas Boulevard. The driver of the patrol car— an eagle-eyed white man with a flushed pink face—stared at Esco's car for one long, heart-stopping moment, and Tammy thought for sure the cop was about to pull up on them. Then he hit his lights, made a hard right onto Albany, and sped off down the street.

"Fuck this shit," Esco said, downing the remainder of his beer. "We gettin' us a hotel room. Get the fuck away from these pigs before they frame us for some shit we ain't got nothing to do with. Let me take a piss right quick. We can slide after that."

Tammy gave another nod, hoping her smile didn't look as tense and apprehensive as it felt. She checked her phone as Esco got out of the car and jogged across the street to piss against the side of a tree. Markio still hadn't replied to her text, and she wondered if he was still in whatever sunny location he was in when she'd *FaceTimed* him earlier. Was he still mingling with the most famous woman on the planet, or had he made it back to Chicago? Tammy had no way of knowing either way, but one thing she did know was that she was more nervous now than she'd ever been in all her twenty-four years of living. She texted a question mark to Markio's phone and deleted the message thread just as Po Boy turned in his seat to look back at her.

"You hear what happened over there on Homan?" he asked, and before Tammy could open her mouth to answer him, he continued on. "They got in a big stupid-ass shootout. Lil James got hit up, his lil brother—Jay Jay—got smoked. Binky baby-mama—Shameka—got smoked. A police officer got smoked. Some old man who ain't have shit to do with shit got shot through his window, and he died. Fat Boo shot Boadie in the face, then Fat Boo got hit up. Spin got shot by one of the police officers. They sayin' Lil James and Fat Boo might not make it. It went down, on my dead homies. I'm glad we wasn't involved in that shit. Twelve finna be on they ass."

"Markio and his people gon' go crazy about Boadie getting' shot," Lil Devin said, shaking his head and stroking his goatee. "Every nigga who ever crossed Markio done got put in a casket. Boadie might be strung out on that shit, but he's still Markio's brother at the end of the day. A nigga couldn't pay me to shoot Boadie in the face. You wouldn't be alive long enough to spend the money."

Tammy was looking across the street, watching Esco's steaming steam of urine as it arced toward the tree. "Yeah," she muttered vacantly, "Markio definitely a real nutcase when it comes to this street shit. They better hope he stays wherever…"

She trailed off as her female's intuition took hold of her. She felt a presence, cold and hard, and it wasn't the icy snow on the ground. Holding her breath, she spun around in her seat and looked out the back window.

That's when she saw him: a short, stocky man in all black, clutching what looked like a miniature AK-47 as he ambled calmly from around the side of the apartment building Tammy had been living in for the past eight months. He wore a black ski-mask and black gloves, but Tammy knew exactly who she was looking at.

It was Markio Earl, the legendary gang member turned best-selling novelist in the flesh, and he was raising his Draco machine pistol to fire on the blood-red Dodge Challenger.

"Oh, my God!" The words came out of Tammy in a rush. Po Boy and Lil Devin looked back to see what had frightened her, but she had already thrown open her door and dove for the cold, wet sidewalk outside, sliding across it like an MLB player sliding into home plate.

And she was just in time. The Draco's barrel spat flames. An unending burst of fully-automatic gunfire, the likes of which Tammy had never heard, rocked the night like thunder from the heavens. She scrambled forward on the elbows of her leather jacket, wincing involuntarily as she threw a glance over her shoulder.

The masked man was right up on the passenger's door, shooting into the shiny red sports car. And across the street, Esco was hauling ass, sprinting off down Albany in the very same direction the CPD patrol can had gone moments earlier.

But there was a dark shadow of a man hot on his trailnow; two dark figures, actually, and they were carrying black handguns with large black drum magazines. Tammy stood up and watched, her eyes widening with dread as they raised their pistols. An insanely rapid rattle of gunfire ensued. Esco fell forward onto the sidewalk and slid a couple of feet. He didn't move after that, but the two dark-clothed figures ran down on him anyway. It looked like they were taking aim at the back of his head when they made it to him, but Tammy averted her petrified gaze and ran into her apartment building before the last rattle of gunshots drummed across the dark street.

Chapter 8

Following their raucous bout of sexual enlightenment, Markio and Nikkia had slept for more than an hour. Then the unceasing ringing of Markio's phones became too much, and he'd rolled groggily out of bed and rifled through his joggers to answer the calls. But before he could even locate his two smart phones, Kay and Buck had started pounding on the bedroom door.

"Lil cuzzo," Buck had yelled through the door. "Shit just went silly at the crib. Boadie got shot in the face right across the street from my…"

The rest had gone in one ear and out the other. Forty minutes later they were back on Gulfstream, and three hours after that, Markio and his two cousins were racing away from the private hanger in two Hertz rental cars.

The police and FBI, having witnessed numerous known gang members running out of Buck's house during the shooting, had begun to search his home. When Markio drove past on 16th Street in his rented black Chevy Malibu, with Kay and Buck trailing behind him in a dark blue Nissan Maxima, he'd seen several white men in blue FBI blazers walking out of Buck's house with boxes and bags of seized property. Fearing the police would likely hit Kay's place next, they'd driven to Boadie's house, which was where they were, plotting and strategizing (and ignoring the incoherent ramblings of Boadie's girlfriend—Tasha), when Markio received the text message from Tammy.

They'd taken Kedzie to 13th Street and turned east, parking a block behind the apartment building Tammy lived in at the corner of Douglas and Albany. From there they'd walked, yanking down their ski-masks as they marched forward on Albany Street's cracked and warped sidewalk, the snow crunching under their black Christian Dior winter boots. Markio had peeked his head around the corner of the building and gasped when he spotted the slowly approaching CPD patrol car. He'd ducked out of sight and pressed his back flat against the building's redbrick exterior wall, and his cousins had done the same. When he peeked again a few seconds later, the cop car was nowhere in sight, and Esco was crossing the street on foot.

"Y'all get Esco. I don't want nobody accidentally shootin' Tammy," Markio had said.

And then he'd popped out from beside the building and ran up on the clean red Challenger, one side of his mouth rising in a nefarious grin as he watched Tammy execute an incredible dive from the backseat. The 7.62 millimeter rifle rounds had punched large holes in Lil Devin and Po Boy's heads, emptying their skulls of brain matter. Afterward, he'd glanced back at Tammy and only got a brief glimpse of her red leather jacket as she vanished into the apartment building.

That was ten minutes ago. Now, as they took 16th Street back to Boadie's house, Markio took his time cruising past Homan Avenue. The cops had the whole block lit up, making it easy for him to see that several of the vehicles parked along the curb were dotted with bullet holes. Fat Boo's X6 had more holes than a vegetable strainer. Little red cones marked the dozens upon dozens of spent shell casing that littered the ground from one end of the block to the other. There were police officers and FBI agents everywhere, including in the air; the distinctive *chop-chop-chop* of a helicopter's rotor thumped by overhead as Markio drove on.

He swiveled his head in the other direction and looked south as he passed Trumbull Avenue. There were a lot of cars and SUVs parked along the street, and people were standing outside in front of the Patterson family building—a lot of people.

It took evey ounce of restraint Markio possessed to keep himself from jumping out and opening fire on the crowd. He wanted Fat Boo dead—the same went for everyone in Fat Boo's circle—but this was no time for retaliation. The neighborhood was flooded with police, and he'd just put two fresh bodies on his Draco, creating yet another crime scene and giving the police another reason to pull over every street nigga they saw.

When they made it to 16th and Millard Avenue, where Boadie lived, Markio parked in front of the house and brought out both of his phones. On his trap phone, his guy—Reggie—had texted him saying their boy—Fat Jerm—had just paid him $38,000 for a kilo of the uncut cocaine that had arrived earlier. Markio texted back a thumbs up emoji. The King Squad Twins had texted saying they were on their way to Chicago and wanted to link up with him; Markio typed, '*Bad time, bruh. Shit crackin' out here right now,*' and sent it. Small Body had texted back saying he could pay for fifty bricks of coke right away if he could get them for $32,000 a piece, so Markio sent him Reggie's phone number along with the message, '*Hit my nigga Reggie, he'll get you straight. Tell Fatty and Stix I said wuddup too.*' Fatty and Stix were two up-and-coming rappers from 40th and Boulevard in Indianapolis, and Small Body was one of their big homies.

On Markio's family phone, Nikkia had called twice already, so he *FaceTimed* her and placed the iPhone in a smart phone holder that was attached to the Malibu's center console. He put in his AirPods and listened as Nikkia told him everything she'd learned about Boadie's condition. Boadie was currently undergoing treatment at Northwestern

Memorial's Level One Trauma Center. He'd been shot through the jaw, the hand, the forearm, and the knee, but he was in stable condition and expected to make a full recovery.

When Markio looked up from his phones, he saw that Bam's blacked-out Rolls-Royce Cullinan had just rounded the corner onto Millard Avenue, followed closely by a CPD Tahoe. Which made for a tricky situation. The biggest threat to Markio's existence was approaching from the rear, but there was no way he could start shooting with an SUV full of police mere feet away. Not even Nikkia Staples could beat that case.

The Cullinan pulled over behind Buck's rental car; the CPD Tahoe rolled past, and Markio saw that there were two policemen inside of it as it pulled to the curb a few car-lengths ahead of him. He'd taken the 70-round drum out of his Draco, tossing it in the duffel bag on the back seat, and he'd slammed in a 50-round banana clip before placing the machine pistol flat on his seat. He was sitting on it, trying to decide whether he should conceal it in his black Dior jogging pants, or slide it under his seat and get out of the car before the police could jump out and catch him with the murder weapon.

Putting his freedom first, he wedged the Draco under his seat, ended the video call with Nikkia, stepped out of the Malibu, and walked around to the sidewalk, comforted by the heavy feel of the twin Glocks in the shoulder-holsters under his arms. Zipping up his black leather Dior jacket, he flicked his eyes from the Tahoe to the Cullinan. He watched Buck and Kay get out of their rental car and cautiously approach Bam's luxury SUV. Kay said something to Bam's front-seat passenger, his yellow face already growing red from the cold as he spoke. He turned and waved for Markio to join him, and as Markio walked to the Cullinan, he saw that Bam was in the driver's seat and an even higher ranking TVL was in the passenger's seat beside him.

It was Fat Man, AKA Fats, a Supreme Elite for the TVL gang, the highest ranking member in the city. He was dark brown and serious-looking in a puffy gray Moncler coat. He motioned with his finger for Markio to get in the backseat.

Reluctantly, Markio pulled open the rear suicide door and climbed in. "How y'all end up getting followed by twelve?" he asked, tugging his jacket zipper down a couple of inches.

"Fuck twelve," Fats snarled "You know y'all both bogus, right? Y'all know all this shit wasn't ever supposed to happen. We T's, nigga! How in the fuck is we goin' at each other?"

"Binky slid past like he was on that. I take my life seriously," Markio explained. He felt like he was a kid again, sitting in the principal's office for fighting some fuck-boy in class. He was outranked by both of the men seated before him, and neither man looked happy to see him.

"You should've called Bam," Fats said, turning in his seat to look back at Markio. "You should've done everything but what you did. Ain't no way in hell Binky was supposed to get whacked like that. He was one of ours."

And just when Markio was beginning to feel like he was being singled out for his part in the burgeoning war, Fats turned to glower at Bam.

"And Lord, you bogus, too. Chief status aside, you can't just declare war on no Traveler! Not without goin' through me or T-Fly. You know law. Law governs all events. Why am I hearin' that you done paid Esco to get down on Kio? They say you put a quarter ticket on Lord's head. A quarter...million. Meanwhile, we got Baby Lord still jammed up for that murder mission you sent him on in Indiana, and ain't nobody bonded him out. Ain't nobody bonded Pee Wee out. You got young niggas we done raised in the mob turnin' on each other, pickin' sides, all because you and Lord ain't get y'all shit together."

Bam just sat there in the driver's seat with the dark fingers of one mammoth paw looped around the hand-stitched leather at the lower curvature of his steering wheel.

"Kio, Fats said, sounding much calmer now, "I understand your brother got hit up. Fat Boo and Spin got shot up, too. We can't do nothin' about that. What we can do is end this dumb shit before it gets to a point we can't come back from. Don't make me eradicate both of y'all from this beloved Vice Lord nation, because I'll do it if I have to. Ain't nobody bigger than the mob."

A short moment of silence followed, and Markio was certain the sanctions were on the way. He was right.

"Bam," Fats barked, "you got a five-minute head-to-toe comin' next Holy Day. I'm givin' you a pass this week so you can get your nephew buried, but next Friday, you takin' that five minutes. And Kio, you got—"

"Whoa, whoa," Markio said, cutting him off. "Hold on, Lord. On the gang, I ain't did shit."

Fats turned in his seat to look back at Markio again, and this time his flat brown eyes were narrow slits. It was a wonder they called him Fats; the man was stocky, muscular, nowhere near overweight. Maybe it was because his pockets were unquestionably fat. He received monthly "dues" from every high-ranking TVL in the city of Chicago and all the surrounding suburbs, many he righteously used to purchase drugs and weapons for the Travelers on the streets and lawyers for the Travelers behind bars. The only reason Markio wasn't making those same payments was because he wasn't a Universal Elite like Bam and Cocky Lord, and he didn't operate any trap houses in the city. He was more into whole distribution, shipping hundreds of pounds of exotic marijuana through the mail, mostly to the guys he'd done time with in the Indiana prison system. Hardly anyone in Chicago even knew of Markio's dope operation, and those who did kept it to themselves.

"You had one of the brothas whacked," Fats accused. "You gon' have to pay for that."

"I ain't had nobody whacked," Markio said. "We pulled up on Binky to check his temperature after he drove past mean muggin', and he upped pipe on us. Fuck was we s'posed to do? That was self-defense."

Fats paused, and Markio fought back a winning grin. Markio knew Vice Lord law front and back, every loophole, and he knew there was no way he could be violated for defending himself against a threat. He also knew that Jock was the only credible witness to Binky's murder, and that getting Jock to make a few minor changes to his account of the shooting would be a piece of cake.

As if reading Markio's mind, Bam said, "Jock was there. We'll ask him."

"I'll investigate it myself," Fats said. "Kio, if I find out you lyin' about this shit, you getting' a five-minute head-to-toe. On King Neal. And both of y'all need to go out together tonight. If we ain't got Lord unity, we ain't got nothin'. Show these brothas a united front. It's us against the world. Almighty don't like nobody."

Markio was nodding, thinking about Cocky Lord and how much it might cost to get him bonded out of Cook County Jail, when two more CPD vehicles swooped in from 16th Street. Three additional CPD vehicles came racing toward them from the opposite and off Millard. Standing on the sidewalk, Kay and Buck looked left and right, stunned by the sudden flood of police, and then the officers were rushing out of their vehicles, some in SWAT gear, others in regular uniform, all of them aiming their firearms at the two brothers.

Heart pounding, Markio watched from behind the darkly tinted window in back of the Cullinan as his two cousins were arrested. He overheard bits and pieces of the conversation a Puerto Rican-looking policewoman had with a Black policeman near his door. "It's them...yeah, they're the ones who killed the boy on Douglas earlier today…who knows, they may be involved with the triple that just went down over there a few minute ago. From what I'm hearing they're the reason this whole shit-show even started. The shooter who killed our officer came out of a house owned by the taller one over there."

Markio slid down in his seat and hastily detached the extended clips from the Glocks in his holsters. He stood the two tall magazines in the inside pocket of his jacket and zipped it shut, finding himself happy with the end result— there were no longer any notable bulges in the jacket that might lead a trained eye to believe he was armed.

Bam pulled off while the street was still crowded with police; a few police officers actually moved their vehicles to accommodate his departure. Markio's heart was beating too fast to say a word, but he was conscious enough to dip the extended magazines back into his Glocks. He loved Bam like family, and part of him was glad that Fats had intervened before one of them ended up dead, but all this could be a diversion. Growing up, Markio had heard all the stories about the ruthless young gangsters who'd become too violent to be contained, and were ultimately murdered by their own organizations—guys like Yummy, a south side legend, and Monster Lord, the notorious killer Markio had looked up to as a kid. Bam and Fats were two of the most powerful gang members in Chicago, just the kind of men who could grow tired of a fellow member and get him knocked off in the blink of an eye.

Markio texted his baby sister, Shakia. She was on 13th and Avers with their other sister—Mariah. 13th and Avers was the block they'd lived on as kids, and when he told her to come and get him, she said she was on her way.

Back on 16th Street, he saw a number of other arrests taking place. Cops were pulling people over on almost every street. He saw Jackboy and Lamont being taken into custody right in front of Bankroll Reeses's strip club on Trumbull;

some older man he'd never seen before was cuffed and leaning forward against an unmarked police car near the corner of 16th and Christians while three policemen searched his F-250. Bam turned onto Spaulding and pulled to the curb three houses from the corner, parking behind a gray Lincoln Navigator.

"Twelve followed us over there," Fats said, after a time. "They know who I am. They know who Bam is. They had just pulled us over and told us we better get control of our gang before they do it for us. It was crooked-ass Detective Milam. He told the pigs in that Tahoe to watch us. We ain't know they was lookin' for Buck and Kay until the rest of 'em whipped up. On Bo Dilly grave, we did not know they was about to whip down on Lord n'em like that."

Markio only nodded. He believed the story, but the story didn't particularly matter at this point. His only focus was surviving to see another day. He'd upholstered the Glock from under his left arm and was clutching it in his right hand, his calculating eyes fluctuating from one side of the relatively deserted street to the other. He had shared his location with Shakia, and he knew she'd be pulling up any second now, armed with her own illegally modified Glock pistol. With Kay and Buck out of the picture, and his oldest brother Benny living the married life in Houston, the only really close family members Markio had were his sisters and his cousin Huey, Kay and Buck's oldest brother, who lived way out in the 100's with his wife—Dee Dee.

He breathed an audible sigh of relief when, just seconds later, his white Cullinan pulled up alongside Bam's black one. Fats looked at the white Rolls Royce with a glowing smile.

"Yeah, we definitely gotta go out tonight," he said. "I would say Redbone's, but it's way too hot over this way, so I'll say The Visionary Lounge. Bam, you bring Malaysia. Kio, you bring Nikkia. Oh, and speaking of Nikkia, I saw you on IG with Alexus. You doin' big thangs, lil homie. Keep that shit up and stay the fuck out these streets. It's dangerous out here. Three niggas just got whacked over on Douglas and Albany not even twenty minutes ago."

Bam adjusted the rearview mirror until Markio's face was in view, and finally he spoke to Markio, the young TVL who'd been one of his protégés in the late 90's and early 2000's.

"Lil Lord…we gotta drop this shit for real." Bam's voice was shaky; he hadn't called Markio "Lil Lord" since 2005. "You know you my lil brotha. All this street shit to the side, we family, Joe. I hate the optics of us being at odds. It just…it don't look good. It don't look good, it don't feel good, and we gotta end this shit. We both got money. You doin' your thing with the books. You got that bad, famous lawyer chick, and she done plugged you in with Alexus Fuckin' Castilla. We should be celebratin' this moment together. Not goin' to war."

Markio nodded in agreement. He hated the emotion he was feeling deep in his heart. It was the sort of emotion that could bring tears if you weren't careful. Markio had a lot of genuine love for the Patterson family, but it was that kind of love that could get a man killed. No matter how much love he had for Bam, the fact remained that he'd murdered Big Worm, Bam's younger brother, in cold blood last summer, on the same night that his nephew—Tyquan—killed Lil Worm. Binky's murder only added gasoline to the fire.

"On the gang," Markio swore, regarding his surrounding with another cursory glance. "I'm done with the whole shit. You just make sure you tell your people it's over, and I'll do the same. I ain't goin' nowhere tonight except the hospital to check on my brother, but tomorrow night we can slide through Redbone's or The Visionary Lounge in back to back Rolls Royces, you know. Fuck they heads up, put on for the block—all that."

They said their goodbyes and shook hands. Climbing out from the backseat of Bam's Cullinan, clutching his fully automatic Glock inside his jacket, Markio paused a second to study the two haggard drug addicts he'd seen standing outside in front of Buck's house earlier in the day. The man and his female companion were lingering on the sidewalk two houses down, the woman seemingly looking at something in the man's cupped hand. Markio stared at them, thinking. Then he shook his head and climbed into the back seat of his own Cullinan, which had been turned into a family vehicle for the moment, with his two-year-old niece—Marleigh—strapped into a car seat and his six-year-old nephew—Jam—seated next to her. Their mother, Mariah, was in the front passenger's seat, all ninety-nine pounds of her. She was a tiny little woman, the angel of the family. She'd gotten marred on New Year's Eve and had just returned from her Jamaican honeymoon sometime last night. This was Markio's first time seeing her since the wedding, and he felt beyond nervous having her and her children in his truck at a time like this.

"Not the married lady," Markio said as Shakia stepped down on the gas pedal.

Mariah laughed out loud and replied with some slick remark, and Jam said, "Hey, Uncle Kio!" Neither comment registered in Markio's brain. He was too focused, not only keeping his eyes peeled for any signs of an attack but also watching the two drug addicts they were riding past.

There was no doubt about it: the older junkie's gaze was unwaveringly glued to the sparkling white Rolls Royce as it trundled smoothly away.

Chapter 9

The beautiful smile lifting the corners of Whitney Clarrett's pretty mouth during her grand opening was at first quite genuine.

It was 10:14 a.m. when she cut the orange ribbon with an oversized pair of orange scissors, her pearly whites on full display for the dozens of smart phone cameras that were aimed her way. Her three teenage daughters were present, standing beside her with her sister Candace, Voltaire, and two of Voltaire's teenage daughters. Trina, the undisputed Queen of Miami, was front and center with her cousin—Joy—to show support for the woman Bunny XXX had introduced her to way back in September. Among the throng of others were Bunny XXX and her porn star friend—Roxy Reynolds. Also present were a few basketball wives, JT of the City Girls, and several popular social media influencers. In all, there were around a thousand people gathered outside of *iKiss Kosmetics* when Whitney snipped the ribbon, and she wore a beaming smile as she led a small crowd of them inside. Hundreds of customers had to wait in line, as Voltaire had smartly implemented a 150-a-person-in-store limit.

Whitney was galvanized by the many different classes and races of women she saw wandering the aisles of her store. There were ghetto girls and business women, Black women, White women, and Hispanic women. There were gay men and transgenders, straight men shopping for their significant other, grandmothers shopping for themselves and their grandchildren. Roxy Reynolds bought the $289 *iKiss Kosmetics* Lip Kit, and Bunny bought the same thing plus a few more items. Candace (Whitney's sister) and her girlfriend—Tiko—bought up a bunch of merchandise and absolutely refused to take advantage of the family discount. A bunch of Haitian women came out to support Voltaire, and a few of them looked wealthier than the celebrities.

It wasn't until around noon, when Whitney was helping one of her employees restock a shelf with Blackberry Bliss lip gloss, that her smile dimmed and became less genuine, and it had everything to do with a conversation she overheard from a group of teenage girls.

"Did you see the boy in the pic Queen A posted on IG yesterday?" It was a thickly-built girl with a dark complexion, wearing a *Hello Kitty* romper and Gucci slides.

One of her friends, a tall redbone with freckles, said, "Mm-hm. That's her bestie Nikkia's boyfriend. He wrote *The Bird Man* series. My mama reads his books. I read a free sample of one of his books on my Kindle Fire tablet. You should see how detailed the sex scenes are. It's better than Pornhub."

"Yeah, well, you know my sister swears she's an actress ever since she played that zombie on *The Walking Dead*," said the heavy-set one. "Anyway, she knows this big movie producer, Karim something, and she said he told her that boy is about to get his books turned into a movie, and he promised to get her a role in it. He said Alexus is gonna be in it."

A pimple-faced light-skinned girl said, "What! For real?"

The thick one nodded. "You know it's gon' be lit with Queen A in it; she has more followers than Kylie Jenner. Everybody's gonna watch the movie just to see her in it."

Whitney's thousand-watt smile flickered and went dim, like a light bulb in its final throes of illumination. She finished stocking the shelf and grabbed Bunny by the elbow, dragging her to her office in the back of the store.

"Bitch, what the fuck is wrong with you?" Bunny asked. She yanked down the rising hem of her short pink dress as she stumbled along behind Whitney on five-inch Balenciaga heels.

In the office, Whitney pushed the door shut and turned to face her friend, her smile long gone, in its place an indignant scowl. Through clenched teeth, she said, "I'm gonna fucking kill Markio."

"Oh, Lord. Not this nigga again." Bunny planted her hands on her hips. "Listen, bitch, you are winning. Okay, he was supposed to show up and support you and he didn't stand on his word—so what! Fuck Markio! You ain't hurtin' for nothing. That nigga leachin' off Nikkia. You got a whole legitimate business now, a multi-million-dollar business. On February twelfth, a commercial for your *iKiss Kosmetics* will be aired during the fucking Super Bowl! I bet you we ain't gon' be seeing no commercial for those stupid-ass books of his."

Whitney walked around her desk—a large *iKiss* logo with a plate of glass laid over it—and sat down in her orange leather swivel chair. She had on a shoulderless orange Gucci dress and matching open-toe pumps. Her Rolex wrist watch and Cuban-link necklace were flooded with VVS diamonds just like Bunny's, only the diamond pendant hanging from Bunny's necklace read *Bunny XXX* and Whitney's read *iKiss*.

"He got a movie deal," Whitney said defeatedly, "That's why he met up with Alexus. He got a fucking movie deal. That bitch is about to get paid big time. Everything Alexus Castilla touches turns gold." She huffed and growled, balling her hands into fists. "I built him up to the man he is today, not Nikkia. I'm the one who pushed him to get his books typed up and published. I'm the bitch who bought him his first Rolex. I leveled that nigga up, and this is the thanks I get."

Whitney's voice began to crack. Tears welled up along her lashy eyelids, threatening to cascade down her sexy yellowish-brown visage. Bunny came around and stood behind her, massaging her bare shoulders and listening as Whitney poured out her frustrations.

"You just don't understand, Bunny. I did so much for that man. Niggas wanted to kill him when he got out. Do you know how many niggas he beat up and shot before he went to prison? How many niggas he stomped out in the county jail? They didn't forget about that shit. I talked so many niggas out of fuckin' him up. And for what? I should've just let them shoot him in his big-ass head."

"That nigga must got some good-ass dick," Bunny said, out of nowhere. "He got you whipped."

Whitney burst out laughing. "Get off me." Whitney threw Bunny's hands off her shoulders, unable to cease the laughter. "Get away from me, Bunny."

"Bitch, I'm serious. You just be findin' reasons to be mad at that nigga." Bunny went back around to the front of Whitney's desk and began studying the wall-mounted camera monitors.

"I got two and a half million reasons to be mad at that nigga," Whitney shot back. "I mean, he do got crazy sex game. That boy used to have me climbing the wall. I've tapped out a hundred times fuckin' with him. He'll pop a Percocet and fuck you for two or three hours straight."

"I knew it, fuckin' knew it."

"Whatever, Bunny. That has nothing to do with why I'm upset. He owes me two and a half million dollars, and I want my money."

"You're thinking small, Whitney. A bitch worth two hundred billion just posted a picture with this nigga, and you're hung up on two and a half million. You need to be his best fuckin' friend right now. Use him like he used you. If there is any truth to what you're saying about this movie deal, the last thing you need to be doing is pushing him away." Bunny went to the door and turned the knob. "Bitch,

I gotta pee. Think on what I just told you. 'Cause you tripping."

Whitney picked up her iPhone and touched the Instagram app. It took her straight to Markio's page. She'd been stalking it all morning, and now she understood the meaning behind the short video he'd shared earlier this morning.

"Big things coming this year," he said in the video. "I don't wanna say too much about it just yet. All I can say is it's big, the biggest move I've ever made in my life, my dreams coming to fruition. Shout out to all the street niggas, all the real niggas, all the gang members they said would never make nothin' of themselves. I'm doin' this shit for the mob, nigga. Y'all know how I'm rockin', free the bros."

In the video, Markio was sitting on the hood of his snow white Rolls Royce Cullinan with several tall stacks of cash piled up next to him, and a fat blunt burning between two fingers. A bevy of plain-white diamond necklaces encircled his neck, and his diamond wrist-watch was a Patek Philippe. The word *CELINE* was printed across his thick white skullcap and sweater in large sky blue lettering, and his jeans were the same shade of blue. His Louboutin sneakers were white like the hat and sweater.

Whitney restarted the video to get a better look at his surroundings. Markio seemed to be on the inside of some large, cavernous garage. An identical Cullinan was parked alongside the one he was sitting on, and on the other side of him there was a snow-white Rolls Royce Phantom. Polo G's "Gang Gang" played in the background as Markio spoke into the camera. The large piles of cash stacked up next to him looked to be all bank-new hundred dollar bills. Whitney decided that, whether Markio was flexing with Nikkia's money or not, the fact that he was on top of his game was inescapable, and she needed to stop hating him for it. Bunny was right. Whitney needed to stop thinking about that $2.5 million and broaden the scope of her aspirations. She'd probably be making ten times that amount once *iKiss* really took off, and she needed people like Markio in her corner. For the past couple of months, she'd been thinking about writing a rags-to-riches memoir detailing her journey to the top of the multi-billion-dollar cosmetics industry, and who better to co-author this life story than a best-selling novelist who'd played a small part in it?

But, she thought morosely, *What was done was done.* She'd already set Flocka loose on Markio and his crew. Candace and Tika's flight had left later in the evening yesterday, and before they left for the airport Candace had dropped the AirTags off to Flocka, who'd quickly planted one on Tyquan's gaudy green Denali. Whitney had tracked the SUV to a wealthy suburb a few miles west of Flint, Michigan. She'd looked at Tyquan's Instagram stories and saw a short video that showed him and his beautiful girlfriend arriving at her parents' suburban home.

Flocka had tried planting the second GPS tracker on Reggie's brand-new Dodge Durango Hellcat—Whitney had wired Flocka $2,000 and told him to use some of it to buy some weed from Reggie—but Reggie had arrived in the passenger's seat of his baby-mama Tootie's Pathfinder. He'd fronted Flocka a pound of Black Cherry Gelato for $5,500 and shaken up with him (they were both Gangster Disciples) before pulling off from in front of Flocka's apartment.

Whitney was contemplating calling Flocka and telling him to forget about the whole plan when her phone chimed with a FaceTime call from Fat Jerm, one of Markio's closest friends. He was the main reason why Whitney and Markio were no longer a couple. He and Whitney had messed around for a couple of months a few years back, and she'd neglected to inform Markio of the sexual relations she'd had with his close friend. When Fat Jerm finally told him about it, he dumped her.

Fat Jerm was a fat fuck, bald-headed and brown-skinned with a gangster's smile and a chef's round belly. He had a mouthful of diamond teeth that sparkled brilliantly as Whitney answered the video call.

"Congrats on the grand opening," he said, beaming.

"Thank you, Jerm. I really appreciate it. It's been a great day so far."

"Just don't forget about the little people."

"Okay, first off, ain't nothing little about Fat Jerm," Whitney said with a laugh. "What you up to out there? Tell your brother I said hi."

"A'ight, I'ma tell him. I ain't on shit. On break. I'm workin' at Walmart now. Gotta show the government some kinda legitimate income. That nigga Markio got us out here eatin' good. I just bought another old-school. Blubby just bought a crib. Lil Jack just got his grill done like mine, twenty racks to Johnny Dang." He shook his head and lowered his voice to a conspiratorial tone. "I ain't gon' lie, between me and you, I think Markio about to flood the streets with dope. Like it was when T-Walk and Blake was still out here."

Whitney knitted her brow. "What makes you say that?"

"Cause that nigga got zah and bricks now. On my mama grave. I'on know where he got that shit from, but it's the purest dope I ever tasted. Straight drop. And he got bricks, not just *girl* but *boy*, too. That's between me and you, though. You might wanna reach out to bro. I know he'll bless you. Call that nigga."

"Hm." Whitney gave a slight nod, glancing at the camera monitors on her office wall. From the exterior cameras, she saw that Voltaire's brother—Keondre Muck—and his second girlfriend, Yemima Elmsley, had just arrived in Keondre's blacked out Rolls Royce Wraith. Voltaire's Rolls was parked out there, too, only his was the all electric Rolls Royce Spectre; Voltaire was big on protecting the environment, and as a rule he only drove electric vehicles.

On the interior camera monitors, Whitney saw that Voltaire and Keondre were walking toward her office, with her daughter Eva, Candace and Bunny trailing behind them.

"Let me all you back later, Jerm," Whitney said.

"A'ight. I gotta get back to work anyway, congratulations."

Whitney put down her phone just as her office door swung open. She stood up, smiling joyously, and Voltaire swept her up in his powerful arms. He kissed her, and she tasted Skittles on his tongue. Which was odd. Voltaire hated candy.

"What are you doing in here?" Candace asked smilingly. "You should be out there enjoying the fruits of your labor."

Giggling, Eva said, "Mama, we are so proud of you. Ava's showing Grandma the store via FaceTime right now. And why didn't you tell us you had hired Brandon to work in the store? You know how much we love his crazy ass."

"He was on the run and needed a job," Whitney said as Voltaire lowered her back to the floor. Brandon Arnold was a transsexual who happened to be the rapper Trina's biggest fan. In fact, he had gone by the name of Trina for years, and he'd lost his mind when the real Trina showed up outside of *iKiss* this morning.

Still holding Whitney in his arms, Voltaire put his mouth lose to her ear and whispered, "Have you heard from the writer?"

She shook her head, by way of saying no, and Voltaire's eyes froze over. He took a step back. Keondre and Candace continued to heap praise upon Whitney for her successful store opening, but Voltaire only stood there, his expression indecipherable, his fat dreadlocks like an obese infant's legs sticking out from the side of his head. He wore a Gucci ensemble, a button-up shirt over shorts and sandals. Keondre was dressed in similar fashion. It was a hot day in January, something Whitney was still trying to get used to.

Sensing the tension from Voltaire, Eva and Candace excused themselves from the room. Keondre was next to leave, using an incoming call from Russell Wilson as an excuse, and when Bunny tried following him out, Whitney moved quickly to block her doorway.

"Nuh, uh, bitch," Whitney said, pushing the door shut behind her. "You're staying right here with me. You introduced me to Voltaire, and now you gon' help me deal with his crazy ass."

Bunny snickered guiltily and put one hand on her hip. She looked from Whitney to Voltaire and back to Whitney again. Finally, after thirty or forty seconds of utter silence, Voltaire spoke.

"I've sent a few of my boys ahead of us—to get the lay of the land, to purchase supplies we might need. My boy Ronnie found us a couple of guns. And they bought me a machete; you know I love me a machete. I'm ready to go whenever you are."

Looking Voltaire in the eye, Whitney thought it wise not to go against the initial plan. She'd put it in his mind to attack Markio and his crew. She'd given him the coordinates to where Markio's boys hung out in Chicago and Michigan City, and let him know that she'd had an Air Tag planted on Markio's nephew's SUV.

As if sensing Whitney's uneasiness, Bunny stepped forward and said, "Look, me and her can handle this shit ourselves. We don't need no Haitian gang to help us get back at a nigga. I'm a street bitch from Chicago. I've been doing this shit for years."

Voltaire's thick lips drew thin in what could only be described as a diabolical smirk. He put his hands behind his back, lowered his head, and began to pace back and forth in front of the camera monitors, taking long strides in slow, methodical steps.

"There's an American saying: 'Teamwork makes the dream work,' I believe is how it goes," he said, his evil smirk growing a little. "We will work together. My brother and I have invested more than seven million dollars into this company, but it needs more if we are to stay ahead of our competitors. I'll not let some bombaclot owe my lady two million dollars and get away with it. He's a made man. He knows Alexus. His girlfriend is Nikkia Staples. He has the resources to pay, so I will make him pay. It is as simple as that."

Whitney stood silent with her hands planted firmly on her hips. A lot of people said she looked like Amirah Dyme. She was a badass yellowbone with long dark hair and a big round ass she'd had since middle school, though it had recently undergone a slight thickening, with Dr. Miami sucking a bit of fat from her stomach and sides and pumping it into her already plump derriere. Bunny, who'd had a lot more work done, was just as stunning, with just as much ass. Together, they turned heads wherever they went.

Several thoughts converged on Whitney's brain at once, the first being the realization that she wanted no harm to come to Markio because of her. She'd plotted against him, and now it was up to her to thwart her own plans. Secondly, she had to make sure Voltaire didn't see through her scheme to stop him and his Zee Pound gang from attacking Markio's crew. It was a daunting task, one that would surely require some assistance from Bunny.

Following a long moment of strategic contemplation, Whitney sighed and said, "Okay, listen. Here's what we'll do…"

Chapter 10

Nikkia had been handling Markio's business ever since they became a couple in July of '22, but all the royalty checks and advances paled in comparison to the single email she received from MTN Studios at 11:41 a.m. on January 9th of 2023.

At that time, Markio was hunched forward with his two-year-old niece—Marleigh—riding his back, her angelic little voice encouraging him to "Go horsey!" as he galloped past an elaborate painting of Beyonce's *Renaissance* album cover that hung in the spacious second-floor hallway at Nikkia's extravagant Burr Ridge mansion. His nephew, Justin "Jam" Morris Jr., ran clumsily alongside them, laughing hysterically as he tried explaining to his sister that Uncle Kio wasn't really a horse.

On the verge of running out of both energy and breath, Markio was relieved to see his own sister—Mariah and her maternal sister, Shanina—emerge from Nikkia's second-floor office. Mariah's best friend, Jessica, stood in the doorway behind them, and inside the office Markio could see Nikkia sitting at her desk, reading something on her computer. Her nerdy Nigerian assistant stood behind her, reading the same thing from over her shoulder.

All five women wore the kind of smiles that only appeared when there was great news to share.

Markio ceased his gallop and swung Marleigh around to the smooth marble floor.

"What is it?" he asked breathlessly. "What happened?"

Their expansive smiles persisted. In the office, Nikkia swiveled her desktop computer so Markio could see the screen, and he stepped inside to get a closer look. Marleigh chased behind him, her tiny hands reaching up. "No horsey?" she asked despondently.

Jam laughed at her ignorance: "See! I told you! Uncle Kio ain't no horse!"

Markio was only vaguely aware of Mariah scooping Marleigh up as she began to cry. His focus was on Nikkia's computer screen, perusing the email that had just been sent from MTN Studios, a film production company he knew was owned by Alexus Castilla.

His mouth fell open as he read, stretching wider and wider with every paragraph. The legal jargon was a little hard to comprehend, but Markio understood the numbers well. MTN Studios had approved a budget of $270 million for the production of *The Bird Man*, and Markio would receive $10 million plus 9% royalties from all future theater and streaming sales.

It's a great deal," Nikkia said, crossing her arms over the chest of her black designer turtle neck sweat shirt. "They offered seven-point two mill and six percent royalties at first. I haggled them up to this offer and had them add in the option for a sequel if this first one is successful. Which I'm certain it will be. Karim emailed me twenty minutes ago saying Michael B. Jordan has signed on to play Jarvis Malone, and it's looking like it'll be either Yara Shahidi or Janelle Monae playing Kiana Dullen. The rest of the cast will be just as star-studded. This project will be like a modern day *New Jack City* once Karim gets it all done and ready for release."

"Say less. Where do I sign?" Markio asked.

Nikkio gave her assistant a look, and Zia sauntered across the room to the printer that sat on a table in front of a wall of legal books. The Xerox machine buzzed to life, spitting out the five-page contract one sheet at a time. She stacked them neatly together and then brought them over for Markio to sign. Mariah had her iPhone out, recording the epic moment. Everyone started clapping as he signed the contract. Markio smiled for the camera, but his mind was on Buck and Kay, not only wishing they could be here with him at this life-changing moment but also hoping they were given a bond for the murder charge they were facing.

Markio had doubled back to their rental car and broke a window to get to the Glock they'd smartly stashed under the seats; without the murder weapons, the prosecutors didn't have much evidence. Two attorneys from Nikkia's law firm had taken their cases. They'd have a bond hearing Friday morning. Markio didn't care if he had to spend every dollar he had, he'd do it if that was what it took to get his cousins free. The fact that they were his cousins had very little to do with it, though he was a lot closer to his Aunt Carolyn's children than he was with any of his other cousins. The truth of the matter was that Kay and Buck were TVLs, and Markio loved the gang like he loved his family. Just over an hour ago, he'd sent Shakia to Cook County Jail with $150,000 in cash to bond out all the gang members who were arrested following the deadly Homan Avenue shootout. He'd paid $25,000 to Cocky Lord's estranged girlfriend, Tiana, whose name Cocky's Jeep was registered in, to say the assault rifle and bump stock were hers, because a felon caught in possession of a bump stock didn't have a chance of being granted bail. And he already had two of his guys from Michigan City—Fat Jerm and Blubby—en route with twelve brand-new Glocks, fifteen steel Glock switches, and four new Dracos to make up for the guns the gang had lost during their arrests.

Markio had also spoken with Bam for a long while once he made it home last night. Not only had he and Bam agreed to permanently put an end to the beef, but Bam had also agreed to buy thirty bricks of heroin at $70,000 a-kilo, ten bricks of fentanyl at $75,000-a-ki, and twenty kilos of cocaine at $35,000 apiece. Markio had ultimately decided against cutting the bricks before selling them—he had the plug, and he figured it best to get the product sold as soon possible so he could get some more.

Then again, now that he had an actual movie deal on the table in front of him, he thought he might just make his first load from the Castilla Cartel his last load.

The only problem was: he hadn't done any research into the Spanish quote Alexus Costilla had spoken to him during their clandestine conversation inside the Versace Mansion.

Markio had no idea what '*Plata o plomo*' truly meant.

***

A few hours later, half of Markio's family was at the mansion, uncorking expensive bottles of champagne and eating from plates of buttered steak and potatoes catered by his cousin Huey's wife—Demetria "Dee Dee" Earl. After faxing the signed contract back to MTN Studios, Nikkia had made a couple of phone calls, and before Markio knew it, his Chase Bank account balance had risen from $522,439.78 to $10,522,439.78.

When his close friend—Reggie—arrived, Markio met him in the garage, and they sat in the back seat of Markio's Cullinan to talk business. Reggie was a coal-black man, roughly five feet ten inches in height, with a mouthful of shiny gold teeth and huge black hands that had punched on dozens of men and women over the years (Reggie was a notorious woman beater, a disturbing behavior that persisted no matter how much Markio criticized it). Reggie wore Gucci from head to toe, and he'd paid $40,000 for the diamond-encrusted "10th Street" pendant that hung from his Cuban-link necklace. He put fire to the end of an obese Backwoods blunt of exotic marijuana and sipped from his tall Styrofoam cup of iced Lean, and the two of them watched as Blubby and Fat Jerm pulled two large suitcases from the back of Blubby's dark Suburban and wheeled them toward the front of the mansion.

"My bitch just went to meet up with your guy Bam and his people," he said, sucking in a dense cloud of weed smoke. "Had her take a brick of boy, a brick of girl, and a brick of that fentanyl to let 'em test the purity. I know it's good dope. Blubby hit a line of that girl and damn near lost his mind. Jerm say it's the best dope he done had in years."

Markio nodded. His head was down, eyes on his iPhone. "How much money you bring?"

"Everything you done made these last few days. Almost two million altogether. I put that thirty-eight thousand from Jerm in there, and I put in three hundred thousand for ten bricks of soft I'm mailin' to my uncle in Virginia. Your guy Small Body had some fat bitch meet up with me in Gary. She was drivin' a U-Haul. Guess he didn't wanna risk me sendin' it through the mail. He sent the money in two fuckin' trash bags. I can't make the shit up. Trash bags. I mean, it was all rubber-banded, but it was still in two black trash bags. He said it's one-point six million. Tyquan wasn't there to help me count it, so I just threw it all in two suitcases with the rest of the money and brought it here."

"Did he get the fifty bricks?"

"Yeah, the big bitch got 'em in the U-Haul."

Another nod from Markio. He had his own Stryofoam cup of iced Lean, though he'd mixed his Wockhardt with Sprite instead of crème soda. He took a small drink and continued to scroll down his endless list of Instagram notifications. The photo Alexus posted yesterday had made him a household name overnight. He'd gained a good nine hundred thousand followers, including several A-list celebrities, and when he woke up this morning he'd been surprised to find that his account was officially verified. All four books in *The Brick Man* series were in the top ten on Amazon's bestsellers list. It was amazing what a single post from the world's most famous woman could do—well, the world's second-most famous woman; it was common knowledge that no human being could ever surpass Beyonce's celestial fame.

Markio was gazing thoughtfully at the photo Alexus had posted when Reggie leaned in to take a look at it. He licked his lips and emitted a grunt from the back of his throat.

"I got some head from that bitch in the bathroom at the club one night," Reggie said, blowing out a long stream of smoke and passing the corpulent blunt to Markio. "This was way back in twenty-ten, when she first moved up this way from Texas. She gave Craig some head too. That was before she even met Blake."

A third nod from Markio. He placed his phone on his lap and toked on the blunt. "From now on, you can get bricks of that white girl for twenty-five all day," he said. "That's just for you. Front Jerm another brick and tell him he can just pay you when he gets it. And be careful—Alexus said the feds been on me for the past couple of months. They ain't found nothin', but that's only because I ain't as hands-on as I used to be, and 'cause I been using these prepaid phones for business."

"You need to talk to your nephew. That nigga so in love with Taliah that he done stopped focusin' on his bag. Shit, I feel him, Taliah is a bad lil bitch, but the bag come first."

"I'll talk to him." Markio picked up his trap phone and began texting Tyquan.

"They just drove back from Michigan," said Reggie. "Think he went out there to meet her daddy. Nigga talkin' 'bout proposing already. Straight sucka."

Markio chuckled and shook his head. He thought about all the drugs he had stashed at his nephew Tyquen's suburban home and decided he'd have it all moved to a more secure location. It wasn't just because Alexus knew everything there was to know about his drug operation. He was more worried about the FBI investigation. If the federal agency ever learned of his stash house, they might raid it and eventually get Tyquan or Taliah to talk, and both of them knew that the drugs stored there belonged to Markio.

Little did he know, there were two black SUV's full of men en route to his stash house at that very moment, and none of them worked for the Feds.

Chapter 11

Bunny's cherry-red Range Rover led the way, with Voltaire and his Zoe Pound gang following a few car-lengths back in two black SUVs—a Chevy Trailblazer and an Escalade.

Whitney Clarrett and Brandon "Trina" Arnolds were in the Range Rover with Bunny. Trina was in the backseat, talking on FaceTime with some man she'd met during her brief stint in the Illinois prison system. Whitney was in the front passenger seat, her eyes glued to the screen of her iPhone. The tracker beacon from the Air Tag her teenage boy toy had planted on Tyquan's Denali showed that he had traveled back to Indiana and parked beside a house on a rural back road in Valparaiso.

They were just leaving the airport. Bunny had left her sparkling red SUV in the long-term parking garage three months ago, when she'd briefly returned to her lavish condo in Chicago's wealthy Streeterville neighborhood to shoot an adult film for Lucid Entertainment, the porn company she'd signed to shortly after her eighteenth birthday.

Whitney chuckled and wriggled in her seat, as was her habit when in high spirits. "This is it, I guarantee you, this is the place where he's keeping all that money, and all those pounds of weed, and all that dope Fat Jerm was telling me about. It's at this low-key spot in Valparaiso. I'd bet my business on it!" she said it in low tones of amazement, speaking more to herself than to anyone else.

Bunny grinned and lowered the volume on the Flo Milli song they were listening to so she could eavesdrop on Trina's conversation.

"Did you see the picture Alexus posted with that lil light-skinned nigga yesterday?" Trina was asking. "They say he's from the west side of Chicago like you."

"Yeah, I know that nigga," the unknown man replied. "After I got outta prison in Illinois I ended up catchin' that bullshit rape case in Terre Haute, Indiana. I ran into Markio at Branchville prison. They called him Chucky Lord in there. We linked 'cause we were both Travelers from the Raq, but I ain't talked to the nigga since I got out. I'm lookin for him right now though. A nigga just offered me a quarter million to whack him. I been stalkin' his page since yesterday."

"Whaaat!" Trina exclaimed, dramatically tossing the long, straight blond hair of her lace-front wig over one shoulder. "They put a quarter million dollars on his head? What he do? And why are you talkin' about taking the hit if y'all in the same gang?"

"Same game, different sets. I'm from off California and Polk. He from 15th Street. Two different neighborhoods. And I don't know what he did, but I know it's crackin' over there where he from. They shot two police in a shootout on Homan last night and one of 'em died. I heard his brotha, Boadie, got shot in the head too, and two of his cousins got jammed for killin' Binky yesterday morning—they whacked Lord right in front of my baby mama crib."

"So who put the money on Markio head?"

"Can't tell you all that. That's nation business. What's up with you, though? When can I pull up on you?"

"I'll be in town for a day or two. I'ma text you my location later tonight, and—"

Bunny turned the music back up when Trina's conversation turned sexual. Personally, she abhorred down-low men, but now was not time to ponder likes and dislikes. Things between her and Keondre were beginning to sour—

he hated that she had sex with other men for a living, and she was tired of arguing with him about it—so now she was searching for her next big come-up.

And who better to latch on to than Markio Earl?

He was the man of the hour, a number one best-selling author who had somehow befriended Alexus Castilla. During their first-class flight from Miami, Bunny had checked Markio's IG page and saw that he now had the highly coveted blue checkmark next to his name. According to Whitney, he was a real street nigga with big dick energy, and Bunny wanted to experience some of that energy for herself. Whitney's plan was to talk Markio into meeting up with them somewhere in Chicago while Voltaire and his gang robbed Markio's stash house in Indiana. It was a dumb plan, but Bunny was confident that she'd be able to reel Markio in if she got close enough to whisper in his ear, so she was going along with the plan, albeit for her own selfish reasons.

When Trina ended the call with her sneaky link, Whitney shut off the music, took a deep, settling breath, and said, "Okay, y'all, I need complete silence. I'm about to call Markio, and I need y'all to just shut up and listen to a master at work.

Trina leaned in between the front seats. "Wait. Let me tell you this first. I just talked to my boo Vontrell, and he told me somebody got a quarter million on Markio's head. He's tryna collect on it. Maybe you can use that to regain Markio's trust."

"I can and I will," Whitney replied.

"Bitch, you are so cut-throat," Bunny said, shaking her head and shooting a quick side-eye at her conniving friend.

Whitney shrugged and said, "It's a cut-throat business. I'm just adapting to it." Then she *FaceTimed* Markio and waited for him to answer.

***

Markio was standing at a tall widow on the second floor of Nikkia's mansion, watching his sister Mariah's matte black Volkswagen Tiguan trundle down the long driveway ahead of Shakia's black Jeep Compass, when one of his smart phones began to ring in his pocket.

He almost ignored the call, figuring it was likely just another random person calling to ask him questions about Alexus (*"What all did she say?"* and *"Did she introduce you to Blake too? And: "Did you get her phone number? Please tell me you got her phone number."*), but when he took out his iPhone, he saw that it was Whitney calling.

He hesitated. He turned and looked down the long, well lit hallway. There was no one upstairs but him. Nikkia and a few of her close friends—Attorney Britney Bostic, Dr. Melanie Farr, and two other well-to-do Black women—were still downstairs in the sitting room, drinking scotch and talking, but all of Markio's people were gone. Mariah and Shakia had a funeral to attend—some sixteen-year-old kid they knew from church had taken eight bullets to the head last week—and the rest of the family had jobs and kids and spouses that required their undivided attention.

"Awww, fuck it," Markio muttered, and answered the video call as he turned back to the ten-foot-high-window,

Whitney's pretty face appeared on his phone screen like a mirage, lively and glowing.

"What the fuck do you want?" There was no venom in Markio's tone. It was merely a question. He tried and failed to repress a wide, toothy smile. "Didn't I tell you not to call my phone no more?"

"That's no way to answer a phone call," Whitney said, beaming.

"Don't get hung up on," Markio threatened.

Whitney sighed heavily. "I'm sorry, Markio. I really am. I know I may have come across as rude and disrespectful the last time we spoke, and I sincerely apologize for that. You paid for that storage locker with your own hard-earned money, and I had no right to demand half of what was rightfully yours. That was very ignorant of me and I apologize from the bottom of my heart."

Markio was gazing down at Dr. Farr's snow-white Lamborghini Urus, and at Britney Bostic's snow-white Mercedes Maybach, and he wondered if their knack for driving white vehicles had anything to do with their friend Alexus Castilla, who was known to have a fleet of snow-white foreign cars and trucks.

His mind flitted back to Whitney. He considered her apology and mentally declined it. He'd loved her with all his heart when they were together, but the burglary at his old Michigan City home had made him think differently about her. He still loved her, but the trust was gone. Now he found himself overanalyzing her every text and call, trying to sense if she was up to something shady.

And right now, all the alarms in his head were going off. *Don't trust this bitch*, he told himself. *She on some bullshit. She ain't never called to apologize before. Why now?*

He sipped from his Styrofoam cup and looked down at his phone screen. "I forgive you," he said, not meaning it at all. "I ain't even thinkin' about that shit. I just got a movie deal. I got ten M's in the bank and ten M's in the streets. I'm up."

"And I'm proud of you. I'm not asking for a dime of your money. Don't' get me wrong, I'd be over the moon if you gave me a product placement for *iKiss* in that movie—support Black business, you know—but I'm cool with just being cool and cordial with you. I just don't want you hating me and me hating you. We've been through too much to be ignoring each other. I ain't gon lie, I did tell Flocka about the suitcases, but I never told him to break in your house to get 'em. I was crying in my room the night we broke up and he came in and sat with me, and I accidentally said too much."

"You prob'ly accidentally fucked that nigga too, huh?" Markio asked, a tinge of jealousy sharpening his words.

"Hell no!" Whitney snapped. "Come on now, Markio. Don't do me. That boy is my son's age. He's actually dating Ava now. He came in my room that night and we talked and I said more than I should have. That's how he knew about the suitcases. But anyway, I really do apologize, and I was hoping we could meet up while I'm here in Chicago, so we can talk face to face."

Markio knitted his brow. The alarms in his head were blaring now, deafening in their persistence. Why would Whitney be in Chicago when she had just opened a store in Miami? It wasn't all that inconceivable, but something about it made Markio feel uneasy.

"I know what you're thinking," she said. She'd always been good at that. "I just opened my *iKiss* store, and I'm already traveling. Well, Bunny has a condo in Streeterville, and she wanted to spend the night at her own place for once. She needs some time away from Keondre. They've been arguing a lot lately. I figured I'd come and stay at least one night with her. Can't just leave my girl hangin'."

"Hm." Markio sipped. Something was definitely up. He had no idea what it was, but it was something. He placed his cup on the window sill and took out his other smart phone. His trap phone. He typed out a quick message and sent it. Thought for a second, then typed out another message and sent it to a different number.

"Plus," Whitney added, "Bunny wants you to sign her books. She has the first three books in *The Bird Man* series."

Markio used his trap phone to log onto Pornhub. He had Bunny XXX's page bookmarked. Hands down, she was his and Nikkia's favorite porn star. No woman on the planet could suck dick better than Bunny XXX. When Markio masturbated, he did it while watching Bunny XXX. She was a sex goddess in his household, and there was no way he was going to pass up an opportunity to meet her in person.

"I'm going out tonight to celebrate my movie deal," Markio said, pressing *play* on a Bunny XXX blowjob video that had already been viewed more than eleven million times. "I'll be at my lil cousin's strip club on 16th and Trumbull. *Redbone's*. Just meet me there at around ten o'clock."

"Wait," Whitney said quickly. "16th and Trumbull? Is that on the west side?"

"Yeah. Why?" Markio took another sip of Lean, squinting cautiously at the panicked expression on Whitney's pretty face. He saw that there was someone sitting behind her, a woman with long blond hair and long white-tipped fingernails.

"Somebody has some money on your head," Whitney said. "Some boy named Vontrell just told Trina about it He said he's been stalking your page since yesterday because somebody offered him a quarter million dollars to kill you. He's a TVL from the west side too, he's just from a different neighborhood. California and something."

Markio nodded, slowly and deliberately, and a small grin lifted one side of his mouth. "I'll see you at Redbone's" he said, and ended the call.

***

Tyquan was pacing back and forth across the tiled floor in his large kitchen, vaping nicotine and spewing great plumes of smoke out of his mouth and nose, clutching a Mini Draco with a 100-round-double-drum magazine in one hand and ruminating over the text message he'd just received from Uncle Markio, when Reggie and Fat Jerm walked through the back door.

"Where Taliah?" Reggie asked, stomping snow off his Gucci boots.

"In the shower." Tyquan looked at the two men, his gaze lingering on Jerm as the fat man reached for the box of

Hostess cupcakes on top of the fridge. "I thought my uncle said not to bring no other niggas over here?"

"Come on," Reggie said, shaking the ring of keys in his hand as he headed toward the basement door. "We gotta get all that shit packed back into the boxes."

Tyquan gritted his teeth at the sight of the keys. He hated that Reggie had keys to the basement and he didn't. It showed that Uncle Markio didn't really trust him at all. Reggie was of no relation to the family and he was a fucking Gangster Disciple, yet he had a key and Tyquan didn't.

They started down the sturdy new basement stairs, Reggie in front with his Glock in hand, Tyquan in the middle, Fat Jerm in the rear, his jaws working overtime on the whole cupcake he'd stuffed in his mouth, dark brown crumbs tumbling down from the corners of his lips and rolling off the front of his gray leather Amiri jacket.

"I really don't understand my uncle," Tyquan complained. "He acts like I don't listen. When he told me to cut Flocka and Benji off, I did that shit with no hesitation. Yet he still don't trust me." He glanced back over his shoulder at Fat Jerm and sneered. "Don't eat all my fuckin' cupcakes."

"Fuck you," Jerm replied in a chocolate spray of spittle.

The basement was a large square cinderblock room with two windows high up on each wall. A single light bulb and a beaded string hung down from the center of the ceiling. The windows were painted black to keep anyone from looking in. Reggie yanked on the string, the room lit up, and Fat Jerm gawked at the hundreds of vacuum-sealed pounds of exotic weed that were piled high against one wall. A long wooden table stood against the opposite wall, and there were dozens of kilogram-sized bricks stacked on top of it. The rectangular bricks had letters written on them in black permanent marker and were wrapped in colored cellophane. The bricks marked "It" were wrapped in brown cellophane, the "F" bricks were orange, and the "C" bricks were green.

A bunch of collapsed cardboard boxes lay piled next to end beneath the table. Reggie and Tyquan routinely cleaned the basement floor with the bleach and other strong chemicals, but the powerful stench of high-grade marijuana remained.

"Y'all start boxing up the bows," Reggie said, meaning the pounds of weed. "Tell Taliah to come down here and help. I'll box up these bricks myself."

Tyquan took out his smart phone and texted Taliah. Then he went to the text message he'd received from Uncle Markio and reread it for the umpteenth time this hour:

'Sending Regg to help you pack up all the merch. Keep an eye on the cameras. Jock boys might be en route.'

Tyquan cringed. He'd been shot in the gut in an attempted home invasion last summer. It was the scariest, most traumatizing moment of his life, and the possibility of it happening again unnerved him. He checked the Ring Home Security app on his phone and studied the live video feeds from all four exterior cameras. There was a white box truck parked next to his Denali; that he assumed Reggie and Jerm had arrived in. Nothing else but road and trees and corn fields for miles in either direction.

He packed his phone, took off his Dior hoodie, and began packing pounds of weed into a cardboard box, keeping his Draco within arm's reach on the floor next to him.

Chapter 12

"What are you doing in here?"

Markio gave Nikkia no answer. He was siting on their bed with an open box of 7.62 millimeter rifle shells next to his leg and the 70-round drum to his Draco wedged between his thighs. He wore a pair of black latex gloves, and he was loading the drum with shells.

Nikkia stepped into the bedroom and shut the intricately carved oak door behind her. When Markio looked up at her, she was leaning back against the door with her arms crossed over her bosom, a low ball glass of scotch held loosely in one hand. Her sexy lips were drawn thoughtfully to the side. Her intelligent brown eyes were stringent slits. Her expression was unreadable, but Makio was pretty sure she was about to lash out at him.

It turned out he was wrong.

"I don't want you going on any missions without Kay and Buck," she said, much to Markio's surprise. "They're your right and left hands, your protectors: It's like Chief Keef going out without Ballout and Tadoe, or Bullet Face without D-Boy and Meach. You need them. You should at least wait until we get them out of jail."

Markio shook his head. "It can't wait, baby."

"Well, what about Jerm and Reggie? Can't you call them back over here."

"They're dong some'n for me right now. I got some help on the way, though. My lil cousins—Tito and Bankroll

Reese—gon' slide with me. Plus, I got the Lords in the hood. I'll be good, baby. Trust me on this one."

"No, Markio." Nikkia moved off the door and crossed the room to him. He looked up from his drum magazine when he saw her spiked Louboutin heels between his Louboutin sneakers, and she took his chin in her delicate brown hand, "Look at me," she said and lifted his head.

Markio set the drum aside, and for a long silent moment they stared into each other's eyes. She maintained eye contact as she took a small drink from her glass. The scent of scotch was heavy on her breath, and Markio could tell by the red veins on the whites of her eyes that she'd smoked a joint or two with her girls.

"Britney's losing her vision," she said, after a time. "It's the diabetes. She's almost completely blind in one eye and the other eye is going too. She's retiring from the firm. I just about cried myself into a coma when she told us."

"Damn. Sorry to hear that, baby." Markio really meant it. He'd gone to elementary school with Britney and Nikkia, and though he'd always had a crush on Nikkia, it was Britney who'd hooked him up with Kisha, one of his first girlfriends. Knowing that Britney was suffering from diabetes sent a painful wave of emotion through his heart. He sighed, shook his head, and again said, "Damn."

Nikkia turned and sat sideways across his lap. She rested her jaw on his head, and he hugged her close. "I'm losing my closest friend in the legal business," she said quietly. "I don't want to lose my man too."

Markio wasn't sure how to respond to that, so he said nothing. Vontrell Maxwell had to die, and there was no way Markio was going to let him live to see tomorrow's sunrise. He'd done time in prison with Vontrell. Markio was one of the few Vice Lords who knew that Vontrell had fucked around with a fag nicknamed Skittles when they were in C Dorm at Branchville Correctional Facility. Not that Markio was homophobic. He just didn't like when niggas played tough and straight in the streets, and tough and gay in the joint. The shit was just weird. And if they were down low and claiming to be a member of his gay, he felt they deserved nothing less than a skull full of lead.

"Talk to me, Markio," Nikkia said, gently stroking the low waves in his hair. "Tell me what's going on."

"It's this gay-ass nigga I was in prison with. He said somebody got some money on my head and he gon' collect on it. I gotta step on him."

"And how did you find this out?"

He hesitated; then: "Whitney called and told me."

Nikkia sucked her teeth incredulously.

"I know she ain't lyin' about it," Markio said quickly." He ran his mouth to Brandon, one of Whitney's gay friends. That's how I know it's true, 'cause the nigga was fuckin' with fags in prison. I ain't about to let nobody live when they talkin' about killin' me."

"I understand your reasoning," Nikkia said with an elongated sigh. "What you have to get through this thick skull of yours is that you have a lot of people counting on you. You just had ten million dollars transferred to your checking account. How much does a murder go for these days? Twenty grand? Fifty? You carry that around in your pocket every day." She got up from Markio's lap and stood facing him with a stern look in her eyes. "You're a boss, Markio. Get out of that soldier mentality and be the Commander-in-Chief. You can't command an army from the front lines. President Obama wasn't in that compound with Seal Team Six when they double-tapped Osama bin Laden. I know as a lawyer I'm not supposed to be telling you that, but you're my man, and I know you're too much of a gangster to go to the police."

"I'll never in my life call twelve." Markio glanced at the black screen of his two iPhones as he took Nikkia's suggestion into consideration. Then he thought of the uneasy feeling he'd had when he was on the phone with Whitney, and he said, "I think Whitney might be tryna set me up. I can't put my finger on what it might be, or how she might go about it, but I got that feelin' in my stomach. She claims she wanna see me tonight so we can talk and so I can sign a few books for Bunny Triple-X. I told her to just meet me at Redbone's."

Nikkia squinted again, straightening her dress. She went to her bedside table and placed her glass on a coaster she kept there to catch the condensation from her drinks. She nibbled thoughtfully at her lower lip, holding her hips in both hands. Finally, she shook her head and spoke.

"No. If Whitney's up to something, she's not gonna try it here in Chicago. These are your stomping grounds. I know her too well. I was friends with her from middle school to high school. She's smarter than most people I know."

"So what, you think I'm trippin'? Think she ain't up to nothing?"

Shaking her head, Nikkia cut a glance at her diamond wrist watch. "No, that's not what I'm saying at all. Business-wise, it makes no sense for her to be in Chicago when she just opened a store in Miami. You're probably right. She's a grimy bitch. I remember when she was dating Black Jimmy, she had him robbed and shot because he wouldn't give her money for their son. She's that dirty. But I don't think she'll try it here in Chicago. Maybe in Michigan City, but all your families moved from there, right?"

Markio nodded. He'd moved his mother—Jeanette—and his older sister—Taquisha—into a nice five-bedroom home in Baton Rouge, Louisiana. Jeanette Barnett was a 65-year-old Baton Rouge native, and she'd been wanting to move back to the glorious south for decades. After the attempted home invasion at her apartment last year, Markio had given her the money she needed to go, and Taquisha had gone with her.

"I don't underestimate nobody."

"Good." She shot another glance at her watch. "I was planning on staying in and getting some work done, but since Kay and Buck aren't around, I guess I'll be your extra set of eyes for the night. And besides—she stuck out her tongue in a lascivious, open-mouthed smile—"I'll get to meet Bunny Triple-X, and if it goes my way I'll have her in bed with us tonight."

"That's what I'm talkin about, baby," Markio said with a beaming smile of his own.

"I'll get Melanie and Britney to come with us under the guise of celebrating Britney's retirement. Let me go and tell them now. I'll be back up in a little while."

Nikkia scooped up her glass and left the room. Going along with her suggestion, Markio made a FaceTime call o King Squad Dre, who'd also done time with him at Branchville Correctional Facility. Dre knew Trell too. A hundred thousand dollars was all it would take to get the King Squad Twins to hop out on Vontrell Maxwell and air him out.

While the phone rang, Markio used his other phone to access the home security cameras at the Valparaiso property. He saw nothing outside except for a white box truck and Tyquan's shimmering green Denali.

When the FaceTime video call began on Markio's trap phone, he found himself looking at a dark red Jeep Track hawk on matching Forgiato rims, and parked at the curb behind it, an identical Trackhawk. "Yeeeeaaah," came King Squad Dre's voice from somewhere off screen. "You ain't the only one getting' to that bag, nigga. We out here."

Dre switched to the front camera and laughed. He was always laughing. Markio couldn't remember Dre's girlfriend's name, but he remembered all the funny videos she used to send Dre when they were housed in the same prison dorm together. They were a comedic couple.

"What's up, bruh?" Dre said. "You comin' outside or what? We out here in Englewood with Crasher. The whole block full of GD's, and me and bro the only two stones."

"I'll be at Redbone's on 16th and Trumbull at around ten. Just pull up on me."

"Bet. Me and my twin gon' be there. You know where we can get some Wock? One of Crasher's lil guys just sold my twin some Trish. That shit garbage."

Markio chuckled. He was staring vacantly at the screen of his other phone, hardly even registering that two black SUVs that were rumbling past on the road at the end of Tyquan's long gravel driveway.

"I got about twelve pints left," Markio said, scratching at the evil Chucky doll tattoo on his right forearm. "You remember Latin King Dillon from LaFayette? That's my plug on the Wock. I get all my pints from him."

"Sell us two of 'em and I'll just hit you back."

"I'll just give 'em to you. Might need y'all to do me a favor too." Markio focused more on his other phone as the two black SUVs came back into view, cruising slowly this time.

"What kind a favor?" Dre asked.

The two black SUVs veered into Tyquan's driveway and went speeding toward the house, churning up a bunch of gravel in their haste.

Markio ended the FaceTime call abruptly and phoned Reggie.

Chapter 13

Voltaire had Zoe Pound members everywhere. Three men he knew from Miami's Little Haiti section—Milk Man, Ronnie Meeks, and Woppo—now resided in the Roseland neighborhood on the south side of Chicago, on the stretch of Wentworth that housed several other Haitian families.

Woops owned a hookah bar and two gas stations, where he employed a number of Haitian migrants. Ronnie Meeks had played power forward for a prominent college basketball team before his knee was destroyed in a motorcycle accident three years ago. Milk Man and Voltaire had been friends ever since they were kids in Haiti, before their parents migrated to the United States. In New York City, where Steven "Milk Man" Carver had spent the majority of his teenage years, slicing a man across the face was called "milking," and that was how Milk Man had earned his name.

The two SUVs were rented under a stolen identity. Milk Man was an expert scammer, and he'd had the SUV's gassed up and ready when Voltaire's flight landed at O'Hara. The four other men who'd flown in from Miami with Voltaire were in their early twenties. They were the men Voltaire sent to do a lot of his dirty work, men with dark skin and fat dreadlocks just like his.

Ronnie Meeks, a close associate of Roseland's Conservative Vice Lords, supplied the weapons: two AR-style assault rifles, a Remington 12-gauge shotgun, a Kel-

Tec 9-millimeter pistol, two 9-millimeter Glock pistols, a .45 caliber Glock pistol, and machete with an eighteen inch lade.

Voltaire held the machete in the firm grasp of his right hand. He and Woppo were in the back seat of the Escalade Ronnie Meeks and Mild Man sat up front, Ronnie speeding through a big cloud of dust as he raced up the rocky driveway behind the Trailblazer, while Milk Man held an assault rifle close to his fat round belly.

Voltaire had no words. He'd already given his men the orders. Two in through the front door, two in through the back door. He and the men in the Escalade with him would be the second wave, entering the house shortly after the first four. He'd studied the location on Google Earth and concluded that there was likely no chance of police arriving on the scene before he and his gang were long gone. There were no neighboring homes for miles. As long as they blitzed the house from both entry points, they'd be able to take what they came for and be back on the interstate in no time flat.

He just hoped Whitney was right about the ducked-off property being the place where her ex was stashing his money and drugs. Voltaire hadn't followed Markio on Instagram, but he'd been watching Markio's page ever since Whitney first told him about the $2.5 million Markio owned her. He'd seen all the icy Audemars, Rolex, and Patek wristwatches, all the blinging diamond chains and the garage filled with white Rolls Royces. He'd seen the video of Markio giving a stack of hundred-dollar bills to a homeless woman on the street, and the video of Markio gifting his sister Taquisha a brand-new Mercedes SUV. Markio was clearly selling something other than fiction novels. Voltaire figured that, if Markio had gotten $5 million out of that storage locker, and if he was the relentless hustler that Whitney claimed he was, then he had surely flipped that $5 million into $10 million by now.

And that was exactly the kind of come-up Voltaire needed. That sort of come-up would make him a lot less dependent on his NFL star of a brother. Voltaire had an expensive lifestyle. All his children were spoiled, refusing to wear anything less than the very latest in designer gear. In the Miami strip clubs, you weren't considered important if you weren't throwing at least ten grand in a single night, and spending even more on overpriced bottle of liquor. Voltaire's all-electric Rolls Royce Spectre had cost him $400,000. His jewelry collections were worth around $680,000, and he owned a wardrobe worth at least $1 million. He'd blown hundreds of thousands on the mothers of his children before he met Whitney, and a few hundred thousand more on Whitney herself. Not to mention the $2 million he'd invested in her company and the few hundred grand he'd put into the renovation of her *iKiss* store. He needed a few million dollars right away if he hoped to keep living the way he was accustomed to living, and his little brother had grown tired of footing his bills.

Voltaire inhaled deeply and held the breath in his thickly muscled chest as the Escalade skidded to a stop. The Trailblazer doors flew open. Four young Zoe Pound members emerged with pistols in their hands and COVID masks over the lower parts of their faces. They ran off in pairs, two onto the front porch, two around the side of the large gray clapboard house

"Well…here we go," Woppo said with a note of finality in his tone. He pumped a shell into the chamber of his shotgun and looked over at his boss.

Voltaire exhaled and slipped on a pair of black leather gloves. Then he pushed open his door and stepped out onto the gravel driveway. He looked around at the spacious country property, feeling the moisture on his eyeballs become dry from the cold winter breeze. He was pushing his door shut when the first cracks of gunfire began.

***

The slide-up door at the rear of the box truck's trailer was open. Reggie, Jerm, Tyquan, and Taliah had already loaded fourteen heavy boxes into the trailer. They were climbing the basement steps with seven more boxes—the boys carried two boxes each, while Taliah carried one—when Reggie's phone rang in his pocket.

He was at the front of the line, nearing the top of the staircase. He went through the open door into the short hallway and lowered his two stacked boxes to the floor to pull out his iPhone. Out of breath, Fat Jerm put down his two boxes next to Reggie's and bent forward to clutch his knees. Tyquan and Taliah stepped around them and headed for the back door.

"Y'all old ass niggas," Tyquan said with an amused chuckle.

"I know, right?" Taliah seconded.

She was a tight-bodied little redbone in Fendi leggings and a hoodie, slim-thick with a photogenic smile and curly red hair. She and Tyquan were in excellent shape. Even with the six-month-old bullet wound in Tyquan's stomach. Panting steadily, Fat Jerm raised one hand from his knew and offered the healthy young couple a chubby middle finger.

Reggie saw that it was Markio calling. He answered, and the wide eyed look he saw on his friend's face told him something was wrong before Markio had even gotten a word out.

"Two trucks just sped into the driveway, bruh!" Markio said it fast, like an auctioneer. "Grab yo' gun, nigga! Hurry up!"

Reggie dropped his phone onto the top of a box and whipped out his Glock, his eyes flashing to the back door. Tyquan had stepped outside, and Taliah was on her way out behind him. Tyquan was unarmed; his Draco lay on the granite kitchen countertop. Taliah's subcompact Glock pistol was stuck down in the back of her pants.

"Taliah, get him back in here!" Reggie yelled urgently.

Taliah was turning to look at Reggie, when two gunshots rang out, and suddenly Tyquan was stumbling backward into the open doorway in a mist of blood, the boxes no longer in his arms. Taliah screamed and snatched the small handgun from her lower back. It was a .40 with a 30-shot clip. No switch. A young black man with dreadlocks and a face mask ran up onto the back porch and stood over Tyquan, aiming a gun at Tyquan's face. Taliah let out another piercing scream and shot the gunman once in the side of the head. He collapsed onto Tyquan and didn't move again.

Just then, a loud thud and a crash came from the living room. Reggie's head swung in that direction, and he raised his pistol. Fat Jerm recovered in a hurry and drew his own pistol, a .45 caliber Glock. His gun had a clock switch like Reggie's. When two men rushed into the hallway from the living room, both he and Reggie opened fire, even as more gunfire cracked in the kitchen behind them. In just over two seconds the 30-round clips in their Glocks were emptied.

The two boys in front of them had opened fire at the same time, but they only got off a shot apiece before their heads and chests were riddled with bullets. One of their rounds went high and wide, punching a hole in the stucco wall above Reggie's head. The second round cut through Jerm's left elbow.

Reggie's alert eyes wavered from Jerm's fresh wound to the two boys they'd just shot down and then to the kitchen behind him. Taliah had taken cover behind the center island and was reaching over the countertop, firing round after round at someone Reggie couldn't see from where he stood in the hallway. Whoever she was firing at was shooting back from outside, striking the wood of the door frame, and the black steel cookware hanging over the island. Just outside the door, in a growing pool of blood on the hardwood floor of the porch, Tyquan was moving around beneath the corpse that had landed on top of him.

"I got shot, bruh," Jerm said, stating the obvious.

Reggie ignored his longtime friend and rushed over to the two downed young men. He ripped the pistols from their warm dead hands and gave one to Jerm, then took aim at the open back door as he stepped cautiously into the kitchen.

"Shit," Fat Jerm griped as he watched the blood pour from his wounded elbow. "That bitch-ass nigga shot me in my funny bone."

Reggie wouldn't have thought it possible that he could burst into laughter in the middle of a deadly shootout, but it happened. He kept his focus, moving forward to grab Tyquan's Draco off the island countertop, but he laughed as he did it.

"Nigga, if you don't get the fuck out the way!" Reggie said, still chuckling as he flicked off the safety on the Draco and tucked the two handguns into his waistline. His ears were ringing from all the stentorian booms. His hands were shaking. He watched Jerm step into the stairwell that led up to the second floor.

Taliah was still squeezing off shots when the gunfire coming from the rear of the house stopped very suddenly. Crouching low behind the counter, she began to cry. "Oh my God," she said, again and again and again. She ran a hand down her pretty face to clear it of tears and rose up a couple of inches to peer over the countertop.

Reggie's phone was still on top of the stacked boxes in the hallway, the FaceTime call with Markio still running. Reggie had just moved next to Taliah, hoping his close proximity would calm her down a little, when Markio shouted a warning that came through loud and clear.

"You got four more niggas outside, bruh. Two with choppas, one with a gauge, and the other one with a machete! Yeah, this nigga got a fuckin' machete. It looks like the nigga that's in all the pictures with Whitney. He climbin' up into the back of the box truck. The other niggas aimin' at the house. You got one nigga rollin' around in the snow by the back porch. Look like he might be shot in the stomach or some'n."

"Shit," Reggie muttered. He racked the slide back on the Draco to chamber a round, something Tyquan had apparently already done, as an unspent rifle shell was ejected and went cart-wheeling across the tiled floor. He thought of the fourteen boxes they loaded into the box truck and instantly regretted leaving the keys in the ignition. "Shit," he repeated with a frustrated forward jerk of his head.

Taliah rose up again. This time she gasped and went scrambling around the counter. Reggie stood and saw that Tyquan had managed to army-crawl through the doorway. The back of his shirt was soaked with blood and snow and Reggie noted two ragged holes in the fabric. Taliah half-dragged Tyquan back around to her spot behind the counter, flipped him over, kissed him on the mouth, and told him: "Just breathe, baby. Just breathe."

"This shit crazy as fuck," Reggie muttered, holding the Draco in both hands and aiming it at the open back door.

But it turned out he wouldn't even have to use it.

Taliah took her iPhone from her back pocket and started to dial 9-1-1, her bloody finger leaving crimson prints on the phone screen. Reggie snatched the phone from her before she could finish dialing. She looked at him, glowering, and he shook his head.

"But he's—"

"We got enough dope here to get every one of us a life sentence," Reggie said.

And then, from Markio: "Okay, it looks like they're taking the box truck. He just pulled down the sliding door and got in the driver seat. You got one nigga with a choppa standin' in front of the house, lookin' in through the front door. The other two carrying buddy who was squirmin' around in the snow. They're putting him in the back of the Escalade." A pause; then: "Yup. They're leaving. They're pullin' off, bruh. Y'all good? Somebody say some'n."

"They shot me in my fuckin' elbow," Fat Jerm bellowed from his seat on the staircase.

Chapter 14

FBI Agent Deborah Wade harbored a special kind of hatred for the Traveling Vice Lords. Her uncles, twin brothers—Alvin and Aaron Wade—had been convicted for killing Neal Wallace Jr., the so-called "king" of the Traveling Vice Lords, way back in October of 1986, when Deborah was just a toddler. In the thirty-seven years since that fateful night, the Wade family had gone through a number of troubling situations with the gang. Deborah had a half-brother who was shot and two cousins who were killed in a home invasion back in 2003. The shooting suspect was a known member of TVLs who'd allegedly targeted the victims over their relation to the Wade brothers. Deborah had an aunt whose apartment was fire-bombed in the winter of 2008, for the same reason. Taking down the TVLs was a lifelong goal of Deborah's and she was determined to get it done.

Which explained why she had gone against Special Agent Jacob Weloby's wishes and continued her clandestine surveillance of Markio Earl and his associates. She and her partner, Agent Todd Pierce, had driven back to the North Lawndale neighborhood shortly after CPD Officer Richard Westman was shot and killed on Homan Avenue. She'd contacted a senior member of the Chicago Police Department and given her eye witness account of Bernard "Binky" Patterson's murder, which led to the arrests of Markio's two older cousins. They'd spotted Bam's Rolls

Royce SUV on 16th Street and followed behind it in their undercover Chevy Van until it turned onto Spaulding, which was when they had climbed out and taken to the sidewalk on foot, dressed like poverty-stricken drug addicts but alert like the veteran FBI agents they were. A few minutes later, they had witnessed Markio climb out of Bam's triple-black Cullinan and into his own triple white one. Which meant that Bam and Markio weren't at odds, after all—if they had been, they no longer were.

It was a public post on Bam's Instagram page that led the two FBI agents to Redbone's Gentlemen's Club. Bam had shared a video to his stories saying he and Markio would be hosting an event at the popular strip club. '*Y'all come out and kick it with me and my lil bro Markio at Redbone's tonight*,' Bam had said in the selfie video. '*Rest in peace to my nephew Binky. Rest in peace Jay Jay. Long live King Neal. We gon T up for gang n'em. Drinks on me.*'

Pierce and Wade arrived in clean black 2021 Buick Envision, one of the bureau's newest vehicles. Wade's string black wig had been replaced with a stylish blond one, the brown stains on her teeth removed to reveal the pearly whites she'd had all her life. The gray mink coat and tight gray Givenchy body suit she wore had been confiscated from the mistress of a south side drug lord. Her make-up was expertly applied, and she wore long fake eyelashes. She was 5,6" and 170 pounds, small up top and thick down low, with rich brown skin and a remarkably attractive smile. The photo ID in her knockoff Chanel bag identified her as 32-year-old Teresa Dunlap of East St Louis, Illinois.

Pierce was dapper in a blue Polo sweatshirt and jeans over Yeezy sneakers. He wore a Chicago Cubs cap straight to the front. The gray in the hair on his head and face had been colored black, and his prosthetic nose had been discarded. His license identified him as 49-year-old Terrance Dunlap. He was supposed to be Teresa's older brother, but they looked nothing alike. Pierce was 6.3" and thin as a nail, with a long face, bushy eyebrows, and an Aquiline nose.

It was 9:12 p.m. when they joined the line of Chicagoans waiting to get inside the strip club. They didn't get through the door until 9:38, and then immediately ventured over to the table near the VIP section. Wade draped her fur over the back of her chair and used her smart phone to make a couple of celebrating selfie videos. Pierce ordered drinks and $400 in singles. A petite dark-skinned dancer, who introduced herself as Kiwi, offered Pierce a twenty-dollar lap dance, and Pierce gladly handed over a twenty. Four other undercover FBI agents entered the club over the next fifteen minutes, as well as several DEA agents who were likely working to bring down Bam's drug operation. Wade's eyes passed over them as if they were complete strangers. She was here for one person, Markio Terrell Earl, and he walked through the door at exactly 10:05 p.m.

Chapter 15

The discernible pain in Markio's eyes was hidden behind the Cartier sunglasses he wore. They were four-thousand-dollar "Buffs." His sweat shirt was black with the word AMIRI written across the chest in letters that looked like blood spatters. His designer jeans fit snugly on his legs, with $40,000 in hundred dollar bills stuffed down in each of his two front pockets. His Amiri sneakers were black and red, like the sweat shirt.

He brought a huge entourage with him: fourteen Travelling Vice Lords, including Bam, Fats, T-Fly, Cocky Lord (who'd been granted bond an hour ago after his ex took the charge for his bump stock), Bankroll Reese, Luke, and Tweet Body; Nikkia and four of her millionaire girlfriends; Mariah and her husband Justin; Shakia, Huey and his son Tito, and seven more members of the Earl clan. They all walked around the metal detectors and entered the building to a round of applause as DJ Pharris announced the arrival of club-owner Bankroll Reese and *National best-selling author Markio Earl.*

Markio forced a weak smile for the sake of the women with copies of his novels stacked upon their tables. On the inside, he was a wreck of emotions. His nephew Tyquan was hospitalized in critical condition. Despite Reggie's attempts to keep the police from visiting the stash house, someone had called them to the property anyway, which meant that whatever Markio hadn't lost to Whitney's boyfriend had been seized by the responding police. It was already breaking news on Fox 32: "Triple Murder in NW Indiana Leads Authorities to Massive Drug Bust."

On top of that, Markio wasn't sure if he could trust Bam or anyone else in the Patterson family. He and Bam had agreed to settle their differences and come together. If that was the case, why was Vontrell telling people there was still a $250,000 bounty on his head? Would Markio end up having to take out the chief of his own mob?

And would Whitney be bold enough to show up tonight? How had she found out where the stash house was located to begin with?

One of the questions was answered as Markio walked toward the roped-off platform that held the VIP tables. He only saw the strippers at first, about five of them bouncing their fat jiggly asses next to one of the VIP tables in the far back corner. Then two of the strippers bent over to twerk, and Markio spotted Whitney Clarrett behind them.

Bunny XXX and Brandon "Trina" Arnold were at the table with her. Whitney and Trina were showering the dancers with hundreds of one-dollar bills while Bunny recorded a video of the encounter on her smart phone. All three of them wore diamond Cuban-links around their necks and diamond watches around their wrists. Two bad bitches and a tranny. And seated next to the tranny with his eyes on Markio and a bottle of Dusse in his hand, was Vontrell Maxwell.

It was then that Markio's forced smile became genuine. He regarded Trell with a gelid five-second stare. He sat down at a table with Bam, Fats, Cocky Lord, and T-Fly. He removed the cash bundles from his pockets, stacked them on the table in front of him, and then sipped from his tall Styrofoam cup of Lean. The strong, four-ounce dose of promethazine and codeine created a numbing affect that allowed him to move past the ache he felt in his heart for his hospitalized nephew and focus on the anger he felt toward

Vontrell and Whitney. He was so focused on the two of them that he hardly even noticed the phone Bam was holding out to him.

"Got somebody on the line for you," Bam said.

Markio looked to the phone, and his brow rose an inch when he saw the pretty face on the screen. It was Bam's youngest sister, 22-year-old Mya Patterson. Markio hadn't seen her since the night he killed Big Worm last year. She was still just as beautiful as she'd been during their brief fling, but there seemed to be more width to her pie-shaped face, like maybe she'd gained some weight since he'd last seen her.

"Hey, Markio," she said, beaming. The song playing over the club's speaker system—Moneybagg Yo's "Blow"—was loud, but not loud enough to eclipse Mya's melodic voice. "My brother told me y'all squashed all that nonsense. I was so glad to hear that. I was mad as fuck about that whole situation. Do you have any idea how weird it was to tell people that my family and the nigga I'm pregnant by don't get along? Starr and Nissa kept telling me to just call you so we could talk but I—"

"Wait, what?" Markio interjected "You pregnant by who?"

Mya laughed at the question. Bam chuckled once or twice.

"By you, nigga. I'm pregnant with your daughter. Remember the condom broke that first time we fucked. Well..." She lowered the camera to the round belly of her pink *Hello Kitty* T-shirt and then brought it back up to her face. "I'm due on the fifth of April. I would've told you about the baby if your crazy ass sister Shakia hadn't broken a bottle over my head in the back of that limo. They jumped me that night. Tinky, Chanel, Kayshawna, and Shakia. Four-on-one."

Markio said nothing. He was at a loss for words. He'd heard all about the beatdown his female family members had put on Mya, but this was the first he'd heard of her pregnancy.

"I admit," Mya, went on, "kinda deserved it. I got drunk at the hotel with your people at the hotel that night and told my brother Worm where your mom and sister lived so he could try to get his money back, and I guess Shakia heard me through the bathroom door. That's why I blocked you and stopped calling. But it's definitely your daughter. Look, call me when you leave the club. I just unblocked you on Facebook. It's way too loud in there."

As Markio handed the phone back to Bam, his eyes scanned the crowd, lingering briefly on two middle-aged women who were approaching his table with books they wanted him to sign, and then on another woman who stood at a table just beyond the elevated VIP platform. She was nursing a dark drink through a straw, wearing a tight gray body suit that accentuated her narrow waist and enormous round ass. She glanced at him several times in a matter of seconds. She wore her hair in a short blond bob, and she had a spellbinding gaze that Markio found hard to look away from.

But look away he did. He signed the books and hugged the fans. He thanked them for taking the time to read his novels. Bankroll Reese organized a line for the others who wanted their books signed, and Markio spent the next half hour signing books, taking pictures, shaking hands, and giving hugs. Every time he looked over at the woman in the gray body suit, she was looking at him, smiling around the straw in her mouth. She had the same kind of plump, juicy lips that had drawn Markio to Mya Patterson, only Mya was a short little redbone, and the woman in the gray body suit was pecan brown, a few inches taller, and much, much thicker.

Markio was so distracted by the woman in the gray body suit that he didn't realize Bunny XXX had joined the line of autograph-seeking fans until she was right in front of him with her three books in hand. She placed them on the table and took a step back, holding her hips, the last fan in line.

"Okay, Mr. Storyteller," Bunny said, showing a smile that looked both sexy and silly. She had nice lips too. High cheekbones, neatly arched eyebrows, perfectly straight black hair. "Sign my books. I want you to write, 'To Bunny, the badass porn bitch I'm about to create some brand new sex scenes with' or somethin' like that. And jot your number down too."

Markio smirked, and his eyes went wide with surprise. Instinctively, he looked around for Nikkia and found her standing a few feet behind him with Melanie and Britney, the three of them engaged in a cordial conversation with Whitney, likely catching up on hometown gossip, as they were all born and raised in Michigan City, Indiana.

He shot a quick glance at Whitney's table and stared at the empty chairs. Then he turned back to Bunny, his generous smile transforming into a petulant scowl, and said, "Bitch, where that gay-ass nigga Trell go with Trina?"

Bunny's pretty lips fell open, but she spoke no words for a full three seconds. "Listen, Markio," she said, at the start of the fourth second, "I had nothing to do with any of that stuff. The robbery was all Whitney's idea. I honestly just wanted to meet you. And Trell said Bam put a bunch of money on your head. That's why Trell wants to kill you. That's all I know, I swear."

Markio turned to Bam. Several other Vice Lords who'd been listening to every word coming out of Bunny's pretty mouth did the same thing. Bam rose from his seat and addressed them all:

"I deaded that shit with Markio. On King Neal. Ask my sons. I told everybody last night that that shit was over with. I wouldn't be sittin' here if it wasn't."

"Did you tell Trell that?" Markio asked flippantly.

Bam swung his eyes over to Markio, looking offended. Then a look of uncertainty came over his face, and he fell into a moment of quiet contemplation. He lowered his bald black head in thought, then shook it and said, "Damn. That's my fault. I forgot to let Trell know it was over. He was the other nigga I offered that bread to. The shit slipped my mind."

"It's cook," Markio said, searching the crowd for Vontrell and Trina.

"They went to the men's restroom a few minutes ago," Bunny said. The fear in her voice was palpable. Her hands were trembling at her sides. Her lower lip was quivering. She seemed to be on the verge of tears.

Feeling sorry for her, Markio went ahead and signed all three of her books, even going as far as to jot down his personal phone number in the third book. She muttered a nervous thank you and hurried back to her table.

Bam promised to have a talk with Trell, and everyone settled back into the celebrations. The DCE Brothers, a popular new drill rap ground, arrived in VIP a minute or so later. Malaysia and Raven came over and started dancing. Another exotic dancer, who claimed to be a distant relative of Da Brat's, said she'd heard from an aunt that the 48-year-old rap legend was pregnant, and everyone gave her the bitch-stop-lying face. The King Squd Twins arrived with their girlfriends and four other Black P. Stones. Markio talked and listened to a few gang members he knew from the area and a few he didn't know. He popped a rubber band off a pile of hundreds and thumbed a few grand onto Raven's back as she bounced her ass in front of him, while in his head he thought up a plan, keeping Nikkia's sage advice in mind as he did it.

He was the Commander-in-Chief.

He couldn't lead his battalion from the front line.

Finally, after several minutes of contemplation, he took out his new trap phone (he'd ditched the other one as soon as news broke of the Valparaiso drug bust) and sent a text message to Cocky Lord's phone, because saying it out loud would surely bring unwanted attention to the issue at hand. Then he waved over King Squad Dre, who was just as short and stocky as he was, and did his best to speak into Dre's ear at a volume no one else could hear.

Dre walked off to talk with his twin and their squad of Black P. Stones, and seconds later the six of them left the VIP section, on their way to the men's restroom.

*** *** ***

Vontrell Maxwell stood with his head tilted back against the light blue interior wall of the handicapped stall, bringing his cigarette up to his lips for a relaxing puff every ten or fifteen seconds. His jeans and boxers were down around his ankles, and his ashy black butt cheeks were clenched tight as Trina's sloppy wet mouth moved back and forth along the length of his dick.

He held his smart phone in his left hand, and every minute or so he'd lift it to either record a few seconds of Trina's phenomenal oral skills, or to check Bunny XXX's TikTok page for video updates. The last video was from two minutes ago. It showed Markio sitting at his table in head-to-toe Amiri, diamonds glistening around his neck and wrists, thumbing hundred-dollar bills onto a bad redbone stripper as she wiggled her fat ass in front of him. The video caused a small bubble of envy to swell in Vontrell's chest, but he found solace in the knowledge that Markio would be dead very soon.

Markio would be dead and Trell would have $250,000.

He wasn't all that sure what he would do with the money once he got it. He'd made no plans. Just having it would be enough. He'd never in his life had a quarter of a million dollars. He'd be the man for once, the big-timer he'd always dreamt of being. He'd get himself a BMW coupé and a brick or two of heroin and take it from there.

He heard the restroom door swing open and held his breath. Trina took her mouth off his dick and looked up at him, using the back of her wrist to wipe a copious amount of saliva from around her lips while she used her other hand to rapidly stroke his hard dick. He looked down at her, biting the center of his bottom lip. Trina looked nothing like a man. She looked like a sexy brown-skinned woman in a tight blue dress and heels. She'd had her ass and titties done, her stomach flattened, and her thighs thickened. A long blond wig framed her cute brown face. She'd been getting looks from other men all night, and Vontrell doubted if either of them suspected that the woman they were ogling was in fact a man named Brandon.

Vontrell tensed up and was just about to come when the stall door was snatched open. He turned to look at the intruders and got a brief glimpse of the men standing there before three of them rushed in and started punching him in the face. They dragged him out of the stall. He let go of his cigarette and smart phone and tried fighting back, but with his pants down around his ankles he had no traction, no balance. Someone took hold of his short dreadlocks and shoved his head down, while the others punched and kneed him in the face and ribs.

He heard Trina scream. Saw her heels run past him and out the restroom door. The blows seemed to be coming from every direction. Someone landed a solid haymaker to his temple that dazed him, made him see a hundred black dots in front of his face. Blood poured from his mouth and spattered the linoleum floor below him. Then another fist collided with his jaw, and his vision went all blurry as he was lifted high into the air. He came down hard on his head, and he both heard and felt the sharp snap of bone in his neck.

Vontrell felt nothing after that. He lay flat on his stomach, bleeding out of his mouth, blinking and moving his eyes frantically about, his entire body numb from the neck down. He heard the dull thumps of kicks to his back and ribs, and saw the boots and sneakers arcing toward him out of the corner of his eye, but he felt absolutely nothing.

It was the most terrifying feeling ever.

Chapter 16

There was a high-definition spy camera disguised as a button on the outside of Agent Wade's knock off Chanel bag. She'd pointed it in the direction of Markio's table and left it there, so that the team of FBI agents watching from a van parked a block away could see what she was seeing.

Having done years of research on the TVL's, Wade knew most of the higher-ranking members by name, and the four men seated around the table with Markio were the highest of the high. All four of them were dressed like Markio, in high-end designer clothing and twinkling diamond jewelry. Their body language revealed a certain level of respect for Markio. It was clear that he was no average Joe. He was a respected gangster like the rest of them, probably on his way to being a high-ranking member himself.

But that wasn't what had grabbed Wade's attention. It was the cold look Markio had given that last book fan, and the way that woman had scampered away afterward. There was something to that. And then, just a few minutes later, Markio had waved over a short brown-skinned man and whispered something in the man's ear. The short man had returned to his own table to consult with an identical twin and four other male associates, and then the six of them had made a beeline for the men's restroom. Mere seconds had passed before a pretty young woman in a blue dress and heels came running out of the men's restroom, and then the six men emerged, breathing heavily and moving hurriedly. They signaled for the two women at their table and then left the club in a rush.

Ten minutes late, DJ Pharris had regretfully announced that Redbone's was closing for the night, as a man had been found battered and unresponsive in the men's restroom. A team of paramedics entered the restroom with a stretcher as Pharris made the announcement.

"Markio ordered that assault," Wade said to Pierce as they filed out of the strip club with the rest of the crowd. "I'm telling you, they attacked that man because Markio ordered them to do it. He whispered something to one of the guys who did it. The guy with the twin."

"We've got an angle now," Pierce said, leading the way through the parking lot to their vehicle. "If we want to get up close and personal with him, it'll have to be at one of his book signings. We both saw how he was looking at you. He's into you. All you have to do is get in his space. Get him to talking. He'll fall right into—"

Pierce went silent and looked back at Wade. She'd paused in the middle of the parking lot and tilted her head a few degrees to the side, studying the fleet of Rolls Royces that were parked in reserved spaces along the side of the building. People were walking past all around them, heads down against the stinging cold as they hurried to their own vehicles, but the two agents stood still and watched as Markio and a bunch of others came walking out of a side door. There were four Rolls Royces—two white Cullinans, Bam's black Cullinan, and a white Phantom. There was also a red Bentley Bentayga.

One member of Markio's entourage—a tall, slender younger man with shoulder-length dreadlocks and a bulge in his sweatpants that was clearly a gun—broke away from the group and came jogging toward the two FBI agents.

"Oh, shit," Wade said. "We've been made."

"Shut up, Teresa," said Pierce. He went ahead to the SUV, unlocked the doors, and climbed in to the driver's seat.

The young man was panting and smiling when he made it to Wade. "Hey," he said breathlessly. "I'm Tito. Shit...I gotta stop smokin' all them squares." He took a moment to catch his breath. "My big cousin Markio asked me to run over here and give you his number. He would've done it himself but he got his girl with him. He the one that wrote all them books."

Agent Deborah Wade's face lit up. *Look at God*, she thought, digging in her purse for her smart phone. "Oh, sure," she said. "I'm actually a huge fan of his. What's his number? I'll text him now so he can have my number too."

Tito brought out his phone to give her Markio's number and Wade was so eager to type the number into her own phone that she didn't see the woman Markio had frightened walk right past her with two other women—well, one woman and one transgender woman.

She was typing in the last four digits of Markio's number when two gunmen popped out of a Chevy Avalanche that had parked beside the red Range Rover three spaces down from Pierce and Wade's SUV. She heard a woman's scream and spun around. That's when she saw the woman in the blue dress, and the woman Markio had sneered at, both of them with their hands cupped over their mouths as they stumbled backward on high heels, backing away from some sort of commotion between the cherry-red Range Rover and a dark-colored Avalanche.

The Avalanche peeled out in reverse, then shifted into drive and went screeching out of the parking lot, knocking the rear bumper off a Toyota sedan as it raced off down 16th Street.

The woman in blue yelled belatedly: "Oh, my God! They just snatched Whitney! They just pointed guns at her and made her get in that truck with them! Oh, my God!"

There were similar reactions from more than a dozen other eye witnesses in the parking lot. People stood stunned by the brazen kidnapping that had literally just taken place right in front of them. One young woman let out a shocked chuckle and muttered an expletive.

It took Agent Wade a few seconds to realize that she'd unconsciously reached into her purse and closed her hand around her plastic Sig Sauer pistol. Bobby Mayes, another black undercover agent, shot her a glance from across the lot, and Pierce stepped back out of the Envision to see what was going on, his own sidearm held down next to one skinny leg. But the show was over. What was done was done. The dark-colored Avalanche was long gone.

When Wade turned back to Tito, she saw that he had already sprinted back to Markio's snow-white Rolls Royce Cullinan. Markio was standing outside the open rear door, his eyes fixed on Agent Wade as Tito climbed in on the other side. He regarded Wade with a smirk that looked more unnerving than intriguing. Then he climbed up into the Cullinan and pulled the suicide door closed. His sister, Shakia, got in the driver seat, and the procession of Rolls Royces cruised slowly out of the parking lot.

Agent Deborah Wade kept her eyes on the Cullinan as it rolled past her. *I'll get you soon*, she thought, with a sneaky little grin playing at the corners of her pretty mouth.

Chapter 17

They'd slapped a strip of duct tape over Whitney's mouth, thrown a black pillowcase over her head, and forced her to the floor in front of the backseats, and while she was down there, with the wet soles of their sneakers pressed down on her neck and legs, they'd tied her hands behind her back. Less than a minute later, they'd abandoned the Avalanche and transferred her to the trunk of a car, and they'd driven for what seemed like an eternity but was likely no more than ten of fifteen minutes.

Then she was pulled from the trunk and walked from an alleyway, through a chain-link fence, up a concrete walkway slick with snow and ice, and into an open bulkhead door that led down a dark stairwell and into the basement of a house. She knew all this because, looking down from inside the pillowcase, she could see the ground around her spiked orange Louboutin heels. She'd have struggled during the brief walk from the car to the basement, but she felt the barrel of a gun against the back of her head, and it was being pressed there with such force that there was little doubt it would be used if she showed only signs of resistance.

Once in the basement, they'd duct-taped her to a chair and left her there. That had been hours ago. She had no way of ascertaining what time of night or morning it was, and no way of asking. No way of knowing if she'd been kidnapped for leading Voltaire to Markio's stash house, or if she was being held captive for some other reason. No way of knowing anything, really, aside from the fact that she was scared out of her mind, and that her bladder was filled almost to the point of bursting.

I have to make it out of this for my kids, she kept thinking. I cannot leave this earth right now. My business is just taking off. My babies are teenagers. I can't leave them alone without a mother. I can't die like this. Think, Whitney. Think.

But there would be no thinking her way out of this nightmare.

Little did Whitney Clarrett know, the real nightmare hadn't even begun.

Epilogue

The following morning, after ingesting a Biggie Smalls breakfast of T-bone steak, cheesy scrambled eggs, and Welch's grape juice, Markio sat at the computer desk he'd had set up in one corner of the spacious bedroom he shared with Nikkia. He typed out the epilogue and synopsis to "*The Bird Man 5: The Last Shipment*" on his MacBook Pro, then leaned back in his comfortable leather gaming chair and *FaceTimed* his sister, Taquisha, to see how she was holding up.

Her eyes were wet and red-rimmed when she answered the call, her hair disheveled. He could hear the incessant beep of a heart-rate machine in the background. Taquisha sniffled and wiped a ball of tissue under her nose.

"You okay, sis?" Markio asked.

She nodded, fighting back tears. "I prayed, and God answered my prayers," she said after another sniffle. "My son is out of surgery. He lost a lung, and they say he'll have a long road to recovery, but he's alive. Hallelujah, he is alive."

"What about the drugs? They charge him with that shit too?"

"I don't know anything yet. I hired a lawyer, and she said they haven't made any decisions on whether anybody will be facing murder charges, but they're probably gonna be charging Kim with drug possession."

Markio sighed. He knew the rest of the story. The Feds had taken over the case. They'd found over two thousand pounds of marijuana and twelve kilos of fentanyl in Tyquan's basement. The rest of the hard drugs had either been taken by Whitney's boyfriend or loaded into the back of Tyquan's Denali after Reggie and Taliah dropped him and Jerm off at the emergency room. Apparently, Reggie had managed to fit twelve kilos into every cardboard box. There had only been a hundred and eighteen kilos of cocaine, twenty kilos of heroin, and forty kilos of fentanyl left at the stash house. The rest had been sold to Bam, Small Body, Fat Jerm and Reggie's uncle in Virginia.

There was a warrant out for Reggie's arrest. He'd fled with an old girlfriend to her sister's apartment in Dayton, Ohio. Fat Jerm was taken into federal custody while seeking treatment for his wounded elbow. Taliah had also been arrested, and Reggie feared she might be cooperating with the Feds.

Markio was more than a little paranoid, but he felt he was safe as long as Tyquan didn't talk. The Feds had nothing on him. He'd never even visited the Valparaiso property, and his drug money—nearly $14 million cash now—was stored safely in the basement of his sister Mariah's Chicago home.

"I am at my wit's end," Taquisha said, lifting her eyeglasses to wipe away the tears. "I'm so glad Jarvon was kind enough to fly up here with me. He has been so helpful."

"Jarvon?" Markio said.

"Mm-hm. He's our cousin Sarah's son. You've never met him. Here he goes right here. Y'all get acquainted while I go and fix my face."

Taquisha handed her phone to a brown-skinned young man Markio had never seen before. He looked to be in his late teens or early twenties. He had scars on his face. Short, nappy hair. Gold teeth like Reggie's. An ice-cold stare.

"What's the word, fam?" Markio said.

"They call me Slime," Jarvon said. There was a gangster edge to his deep southern drawl. He glanced in the direction Taquisha had gone, then turned back to Markio. "I ain't tell Taquisha, but I really left Baton Rouge 'cause twelve been tryna question me 'bout some bodies, ya heard me. We been at war with the other side. Had to get away for a minute, ya heard me."

"Feds been on my ass for the same kinda shit," Markio said with a growing smile. "Nice to meet you, cousin."

He talked with Slime for the next twenty-five minutes. Slime told Markio about life on the north side of Baton Rouge, and how his gang of Bloods had been "slangin' iron" day and night for the past couple of years. Markio told Slime about the federal investigation he'd been under for the last six months. The conversation flowed smoothly and likely would have continued had Nikkia and Bunny XXX not walked out of he bathroom and stood behind Markio's chair, Nikkia in a black-lace Victoria's Secret teddy, Bunny in a pink Versace robe over a croctchless pink Savage X Fenty catsuit. Slime's eyes widened when he caught sight of them.

"A'ight, Slime," Markio said as the two women bent to kiss either side of his face. "As you can see, I got some business to tend to here. Put my number in your phone and hit me up later. You can come and hang out with me. I got plenty money, plenty guns. You'll be good."

Slime showed a glimmer of a smile and then ended he call.

It was the beginning of a deadly partnership the likes of which hadn't been seen in years.

The End

Lock Down Publications and Ca$h Presents
Assisted Publishing Packages

BASIC PACKAGE	UPGRADED PACKAGE
$499	$800
Editing	Typing
Cover Design	Editing
Formatting	Cover Design
	Formatting
ADVANCE PACKAGE	**LDP SUPREME PACKAGE**
$1,200	$1,500
Typing	Typing
Editing	Editing
Cover Design	Cover Design
Formatting	Formatting
Copyright registration	Copyright registration
Proofreading	Proofreading
Upload book to Amazon	Set up Amazon account
	Upload book to Amazon
	Advertise on LDP, Amazon and Facebook Page

***Other services available upon request.
Additional charges may apply

Lock Down Publications
P.O. Box 944
Stockbridge, GA 30281-9998
Phone: 470 303-9761

Submission Guideline

Submit the first three chapters of your completed manuscript to ldpsubmissions@gmail.com. In the subject line add **Your Book's Title**. The manuscript must be in a Word Doc file and sent as an attachment. Document should be in Times New Roman, double spaced, and in size 12 font. Also, provide your synopsis and full contact information. If sending multiple submissions, they must each be in a separate email.

Have a story but no way to send it electronically? You can still submit to LDP/Ca$h Presents. Send in the first three chapters, written or typed, of your completed manuscript to:

LDP: Submissions Dept
P.O. Box 944
Stockbridge, GA 30281-9998

DO NOT send original manuscript. Must be a duplicate. Provide your synopsis and a cover letter containing your full contact information.

Thanks for considering LDP and Ca$h Presents.

NEW RELEASES

BLOODLINE OF A SAVAGE **BY PRINCE A. TAUHID**

THE MURDER QUEENS 4 **BY MICHAEL GALLON**

THE BUTTERFLY MAFIA **BY FUMIYA PAYNE**

KING KILLA 2 **BY VINCENT "VITTO" HOLLOWAY**

BABY, I'M WINTERTIME COLD 3 **BY MEESHA**

THESE VICIOUS STREETS **BY PRINCE A. TAUHID**

TIL DEATH 2 **BY ARYANNA**

CITY OF SMOKE 2 **BY MOLOTTI**

STEPPERS **BY KING RIO**

THE LANE **BY KEN-KEN SPENCE**

MONEY GAME 2 **BY SMOOVE DOLLA**

THE BLACK DIAMOND CARTEL **BY SAYNOMORE**

CRIME BOSS 2 **BY PLAYA RAY**

THUG OF SPADES **BY COREY ROBINSON**

LOVE IN THE TRENCHES 2 **BY COREY ROBINSON**

TIL DEATH 3 **BY ARYANNA**

THE BIRTH OF A GANGSTER 4 **BY DELMONT PLAYER**

PRODUCT OF THE STREETS **BY DEMOND "MONEY" ANDERSON**

Coming Soon from Lock Down Publications/Ca$h Presents

BLOOD OF A BOSS VI
SHADOWS OF THE GAME II
TRAP BASTARD II
By **Askari**

LOYAL TO THE GAME IV
By **T.J. & Jelissa**

TRUE SAVAGE VIII
MIDNIGHT CARTEL IV
DOPE BOY MAGIC IV
CITY OF KINGZ III
NIGHTMARE ON SILENT AVE II
THE PLUG OF LIL MEXICO II
CLASSIC CITY II
By **Chris Green**

BLAST FOR ME III
A SAVAGE DOPEBOY III
CUTTHROAT MAFIA III
DUFFLE BAG CARTEL VII
HEARTLESS GOON VI
By **Ghost**

A HUSTLER'S DECEIT III
KILL ZONE II
BAE BELONGS TO ME III
TIL DEATH II
By **Aryanna**

KING OF THE TRAP III
By **T.J. Edwards**

GORILLAZ IN THE BAY V
3X KRAZY III
STRAIGHT BEAST MODE III
By **De'Kari**

KINGPIN KILLAZ IV
STREET KINGS III
PAID IN BLOOD III
CARTEL KILLAZ IV
DOPE GODS III
By **Hood Rich**

SINS OF A HUSTLA II
By **ASAD**

YAYO V
BRED IN THE GAME 2
By **S. Allen**

THE STREETS WILL TALK II
By **Yolanda Moore**

SON OF A DOPE FIEND III
HEAVEN GOT A GHETTO III
SKI MASK MONEY III
By **Renta**

LOYALTY AIN'T PROMISED III
By **Keith Williams**

I'M NOTHING WITHOUT HIS LOVE II
SINS OF A THUG II
TO THE THUG I LOVED BEFORE II
IN A HUSTLER I TRUST II
By **Monet Dragun**

QUIET MONEY IV
EXTENDED CLIP III
THUG LIFE IV
By **Trai'Quan**

THE STREETS MADE ME IV
By **Larry D. Wright**

IF YOU CROSS ME ONCE III
ANGEL V
By **Anthony Fields**

THE STREETS WILL NEVER CLOSE IV
By **K'ajji**

HARD AND RUTHLESS III
KILLA KOUNTY IV
By **Khufu**

MONEY GAME III
By **Smoove Dolla**

MURDA WAS THE CASE III
Elijah R. Freeman

AN UNFORESEEN LOVE IV
BABY, I'M WINTERTIME COLD III
By **Meesha**

QUEEN OF THE ZOO III
By **Black Migo**

CONFESSIONS OF A JACKBOY III
By **Nicholas Lock**

JACK BOYS VS DOPE BOYS IV
A GANGSTA'S QUR'AN V
COKE GIRLZ II
COKE BOYS II
LIFE OF A SAVAGE V
CHI'RAQ GANGSTAS V
SOSA GANG III
BRONX SAVAGES II
BODYMORE KINGPINS II
By **Romell Tukes**

KING KILLA II
By **Vincent "Vitto" Holloway**

BETRAYAL OF A THUG III
By **Fre$h**

THE MURDER QUEENS III
By **Michael Gallon**

THE BIRTH OF A GANGSTER III
By **Delmont Player**

TREAL LOVE II
By **Le'Monica Jackson**

FOR THE LOVE OF BLOOD III
By **Jamel Mitchell**

RAN OFF ON DA PLUG II
By **Paper Boi Rari**

HOOD CONSIGLIERE III
By **Keese**

PRETTY GIRLS DO NASTY THINGS II
By **Nicole Goosby**

PROTÉGÉ OF A LEGEND III
LOVE IN THE TRENCHES II
By **Corey Robinson**

IT'S JUST ME AND YOU II
By **Ah'Million**

FOREVER GANGSTA III
By **Adrian Dulan**

GORILLAZ IN THE TRENCHES II
By **SayNoMore**

THE COCAINE PRINCESS VIII
By **King Rio**

CRIME BOSS II
By **Playa Ray**

LOYALTY IS EVERYTHING III
By **Molotti**

HERE TODAY GONE TOMORROW II
By **Fly Rock**

SUPER GREMLIN 3 | KING RIO

REAL G'S MOVE IN SILENCE II
By **Von Diesel**

GRIMEY WAYS IV
By **Ray Vinci**

Available Now

RESTRAINING ORDER I & II
By **CA$H & Coffee**

LOVE KNOWS NO BOUNDARIES I II & III
By **Coffee**

RAISED AS A GOON I, II, III & IV
BRED BY THE SLUMS I, II, III
BLAST FOR ME I & II
ROTTEN TO THE CORE I II III
A BRONX TALE I, II, III
DUFFLE BAG CARTEL I II III IV V VI
HEARTLESS GOON I II III IV V
A SAVAGE DOPEBOY I II
DRUG LORDS I II III
CUTTHROAT MAFIA I II
KING OF THE TRENCHES
By **Ghost**

LAY IT DOWN I & II
LAST OF A DYING BREED I II
BLOOD STAINS OF A SHOTTA I & II III
By **Jamaica**

LOYAL TO THE GAME I II III
LIFE OF SIN I, II III
By **TJ & Jelissa**

IF LOVING HIM IS WRONG…I & II
LOVE ME EVEN WHEN IT HURTS I II III
By **Jelissa**

BLOODY COMMAS I & II
SKI MASK CARTEL I, II & III
KING OF NEW YORK I II, III IV V
RISE TO POWER I II III
COKE KINGS I II III IV V
BORN HEARTLESS I II III IV
KING OF THE TRAP I II
By **T.J. Edwards**

WHEN THE STREETS CLAP BACK I & II III
THE HEART OF A SAVAGE I II III IV
MONEY MAFIA I II
LOYAL TO THE SOIL I II III
By **Jibril Williams**

A DISTINGUISHED THUG STOLE MY HEART I II &
III
LOVE SHOULDN'T HURT I II III IV
RENEGADE BOYS I II III IV
PAID IN KARMA I II III
SAVAGE STORMS I II III
AN UNFORESEEN LOVE I II III
BABY, I'M WINTERTIME COLD I II
By **Meesha**

A GANGSTER'S CODE I &, II III
A GANGSTER'S SYN I II III
THE SAVAGE LIFE I II III
CHAINED TO THE STREETS I II III
BLOOD ON THE MONEY I II III
A GANGSTA'S PAIN I II III
By **J-Blunt**

PUSH IT TO THE LIMIT
By **Bre' Hayes**

BLOOD OF A BOSS I, II, III, IV, V
SHADOWS OF THE GAME
TRAP BASTARD
By **Askari**

THE STREETS BLEED MURDER I, II & III
THE HEART OF A GANGSTA I II& III
By **Jerry Jackson**

CUM FOR ME I II III IV V VI VII VIII
An **LDP Erotica Collaboration**

BRIDE OF A HUSTLA I II & II
THE FETTI GIRLS I, II& III
CORRUPTED BY A GANGSTA I, II III, IV
BLINDED BY HIS LOVE
THE PRICE YOU PAY FOR LOVE I, II ,III
DOPE GIRL MAGIC I II III
By **Destiny Skai**

WHEN A GOOD GIRL GOES BAD
By **Adrienne**

A GANGSTER'S REVENGE I II III & IV
THE BOSS MAN'S DAUGHTERS I II III IV V
A SAVAGE LOVE I & II
BAE BELONGS TO ME I II
A HUSTLER'S DECEIT I, II, III
WHAT BAD BITCHES DO I, II, III
SOUL OF A MONSTER I II III
KILL ZONE
A DOPE BOY'S QUEEN I II III
TIL DEATH
By **Aryanna**

SUPER GREMLIN 3 | KING RIO

THE COST OF LOYALTY I II III
By Kweli

A KINGPIN'S AMBITION
A KINGPIN'S AMBITION **II**
I MURDER FOR THE DOUGH
By **Ambitious**

TRUE SAVAGE I II III IV V VI VII
DOPE BOY MAGIC I, II, III
MIDNIGHT CARTEL I II III
CITY OF KINGZ I II
NIGHTMARE ON SILENT AVE
THE PLUG OF LIL MEXICO II
CLASSIC CITY
By **Chris Green**

A DOPEBOY'S PRAYER
By **Eddie "Wolf" Lee**

THE KING CARTEL I, II & III
By **Frank Gresham**

THESE NIGGAS AIN'T LOYAL I, II & III
By **Nikki Tee**

GANGSTA SHYT I II &III
By **CATO**

THE ULTIMATE BETRAYAL
By **Phoenix**

BOSS'N UP I, II & III
By **Royal Nicole**

SUPER GREMLIN 3 | KING RIO

I LOVE YOU TO DEATH
By **Destiny J**

I RIDE FOR MY HITTA
I STILL RIDE FOR MY HITTA
By **Misty Holt**

LOVE & CHASIN' PAPER
By **Qay Crockett**

TO DIE IN VAIN
SINS OF A HUSTLA
By **ASAD**

BROOKLYN HUSTLAZ
By **Boogsy Morina**

BROOKLYN ON LOCK I & II
By **Sonovia**

GANGSTA CITY
By **Teddy Duke**

A DRUG KING AND HIS DIAMOND I & II III
A DOPEMAN'S RICHES
HER MAN, MINE'S TOO I, II
CASH MONEY HO'S
THE WIFEY I USED TO BE I II
PRETTY GIRLS DO NASTY THINGS
By Nicole Goosby

LIPSTICK KILLAH I, II, III
CRIME OF PASSION I II & III
FRIEND OR FOE I II III
By **Mimi**

TRAPHOUSE KING I II & III
KINGPIN KILLAZ I II III
STREET KINGS I II
PAID IN BLOOD I II
CARTEL KILLAZ I II III
DOPE GODS I II
By **Hood Rich**

STEADY MOBBN' I, II, III
THE STREETS STAINED MY SOUL I II III
By **Marcellus Allen**

WHO SHOT YA I, II, III
SON OF A DOPE FIEND I II
HEAVEN GOT A GHETTO I II
SKI MASK MONEY I II
By **Renta**

GORILLAZ IN THE BAY I II III IV
TEARS OF A GANGSTA I II
3X KRAZY I II
STRAIGHT BEAST MODE I II
By **DE'KARI**

TRIGGADALE I II III
MURDA WAS THE CASE I II
By **Elijah R. Freeman**

THE STREETS ARE CALLING
By **Duquie Wilson**

SLAUGHTER GANG I II III
RUTHLESS HEART I II III
By **Willie Slaughter**

SUPER GREMLIN 3 | KING RIO

GOD BLESS THE TRAPPERS I, II, III
THESE SCANDALOUS STREETS I, II, III
FEAR MY GANGSTA I, II, III IV, V
THESE STREETS DON'T LOVE NOBODY I, II
BURY ME A G I, II, III, IV, V
A GANGSTA'S EMPIRE I, II, III, IV
THE DOPEMAN'S BODYGAURD I II
THE REALEST KILLAZ I II III
THE LAST OF THE OGS I II III
By **Tranay Adams**

MARRIED TO A BOSS I II III
By **Destiny Skai & Chris Green**

KINGZ OF THE GAME I II III IV V VI VII
CRIME BOSS
By **Playa Ray**

FUK SHYT
By **Blakk Diamond**

DON'T F#CK WITH MY HEART I II
By **Linnea**

ADDICTED TO THE DRAMA I II III
IN THE ARM OF HIS BOSS II
By **Jamila**

YAYO I II III IV
A SHOOTER'S AMBITION I II
BRED IN THE GAME
By **S. Allen**

LOYALTY AIN'T PROMISED I II
By **Keith Williams**

187

TRAP GOD I II III
RICH $AVAGE I II III
MONEY IN THE GRAVE I II III
By **Martell Troublesome Bolden**

FOREVER GANGSTA I II
GLOCKS ON SATIN SHEETS I II
By **Adrian Dulan**

TOE TAGZ I II III IV
LEVELS TO THIS SHYT I II
IT'S JUST ME AND YOU
By **Ah'Million**

KINGPIN DREAMS I II III
RAN OFF ON DA PLUG
By **Paper Boi Rari**

CONFESSIONS OF A GANGSTA I II III IV
CONFESSIONS OF A JACKBOY I II
By **Nicholas Lock**

I'M NOTHING WITHOUT HIS LOVE
SINS OF A THUG
TO THE THUG I LOVED BEFORE
A GANGSTA SAVED XMAS
IN A HUSTLER I TRUST
By **Monet Dragun**

QUIET MONEY I II III
THUG LIFE I II III
EXTENDED CLIP I II
A GANGSTA'S PARADISE
By **Trai'Quan**

SUPER GREMLIN 3 | KING RIO

CAUGHT UP IN THE LIFE I II III
THE STREETS NEVER LET GO I II III
By **Robert Baptiste**

NEW TO THE GAME I II III
MONEY, MURDER & MEMORIES I II III
By **Malik D. Rice**

CREAM I II III
THE STREETS WILL TALK
By **Yolanda Moore**

LIFE OF A SAVAGE I II III IV
A GANGSTA'S QUR'AN I II III IV
MURDA SEASON I II III
GANGLAND CARTEL I II III
CHI'RAQ GANGSTAS I II III IV
KILLERS ON ELM STREET I II III
JACK BOYZ N DA BRONX I II III
A DOPEBOY'S DREAM I II III
JACK BOYS VS DOPE BOYS I II III
COKE GIRLZ
COKE BOYS
SOSA GANG I II
BRONX SAVAGES
BODYMORE KINGPINS
By **Romell Tukes**

THE STREETS MADE ME I II III
By **Larry D. Wright**

CONCRETE KILLA I II III
VICIOUS LOYALTY I II III
By **Kingpen**

THE ULTIMATE SACRIFICE I, II, III, IV, V, VI
KHADIFI
IF YOU CROSS ME ONCE I II
ANGEL I II III IV
IN THE BLINK OF AN EYE
By **Anthony Fields**

THE LIFE OF A HOOD STAR
By **Ca$h & Rashia Wilson**

THE STREETS WILL NEVER CLOSE I II III
By **K'ajji**

NIGHTMARES OF A HUSTLA I II III
By **King Dream**

HARD AND RUTHLESS I II
MOB TOWN 251
THE BILLIONAIRE BENTLEYS I II III
REAL G'S MOVE IN SILENCE
By **Von Diesel**

GHOST MOB
By **Stilloan Robinson**

MOB TIES I II III IV V VI
SOUL OF A HUSTLER, HEART OF A KILLER I II
GORILLAZ IN THE TRENCHES
By **SayNoMore**

BODYMORE MURDERLAND I II III
THE BIRTH OF A GANGSTER I II
By **Delmont Player**

SUPER GREMLIN 3 | KING RIO

FOR THE LOVE OF A BOSS
By **C. D. Blue**

KILLA KOUNTY I II III IV
By Khufu

MOBBED UP I II III IV
THE BRICK MAN I II III IV V
THE COCAINE PRINCESS I II III IV V VI VII
By **King Rio**

MONEY GAME I II
By **Smoove Dolla**

A GANGSTA'S KARMA I II III
By **FLAME**

KING OF THE TRENCHES I II III
By **GHOST & TRANAY ADAMS**

QUEEN OF THE ZOO I II
By **Black Migo**

GRIMEY WAYS I II III
By **Ray Vinci**

XMAS WITH AN ATL SHOOTER
By **Ca$h & Destiny Skai**

KING KILLA
By **Vincent "Vitto" Holloway**

BETRAYAL OF A THUG I II
By **Fre$h**

SUPER GREMLIN 3 | KING RIO

THE MURDER QUEENS I II
By **Michael Gallon**

TREAL LOVE
By **Le'Monica Jackson**

FOR THE LOVE OF BLOOD I II
By **Jamel Mitchell**

HOOD CONSIGLIERE I II
By **Keese**

PROTÉGÉ OF A LEGEND I II
LOVE IN THE TRENCHES
By **Corey Robinson**

BORN IN THE GRAVE I II III
By **Self Made Tay**

MOAN IN MY MOUTH
By **XTASY**

TORN BETWEEN A GANGSTER AND A
GENTLEMAN
By **J-BLUNT & Miss Kim**

LOYALTY IS EVERYTHING I II
By **Molotti**

HERE TODAY GONE TOMORROW
By **Fly Rock**

PILLOW PRINCESS
By **S. Hawkins**

SUPER GREMLIN 3 | KING RIO

SANCTIFIED AND HORNY
by **XTASY**

THE PLUG OF LIL MEXICO 2
by **CHRIS GREEN**

THE BLACK DIAMOND CARTEL
by **SAYNOMORE**

THE BIRTH OF A GANGSTER 3
by **DELMONT PLAYER**

BOOKS BY LDP'S CEO, CA$H

TRUST IN NO MAN
TRUST IN NO MAN 2
TRUST IN NO MAN 3
BONDED BY BLOOD
SHORTY GOT A THUG
THUGS CRY
THUGS CRY 2
THUGS CRY 3
TRUST NO BITCH
TRUST NO BITCH 2
TRUST NO BITCH 3
TIL MY CASKET DROPS
RESTRAINING ORDER
RESTRAINING ORDER 2
IN LOVE WITH A CONVICT
LIFE OF A HOOD STAR
XMAS WITH AN ATL SHOOTER